The entire rear of the hold was gone,
the hatch torn away, clouds and sky whipping past at
incredible speed. Confused, Claire took a single step
forward—and saw what the problem was.

Mr. X, she thought wildly, remembering the monstrous thing in Raccoon, the relentless pursuer in the
long, dark coat—but the hulking creature straddling the
hydraulic track wasn't the same. It was humanoid,
giant-sized and hairless like the X monster—but it was
also taller, its shoulders impossibly broad, its abdomen
rippled with muscle. Its left fist was a metal-spiked
mace bigger than her entire head, its right hand a
hybrid of flesh and curving knives, two of them at least
a foot long. The monster turned its cataract-white eyes
to look at her before throwing its head back and
roaring, an explosive howl of blood lust and fury.

Terrified but determined, Claire raised her suddenly
pathetic weapon as the creature started for her, and put
the red dot on its right unicolor eye. She squeezed the
trigger—

—and heard the dry *click* of an empty chamber,
deafeningly loud even over the raging winds that spun
past the damaged plane.

RESIDENT EVIL™

CODE: VERONICA

S.D. PERRY

POCKET BOOKS
New York   London   Toronto   Sydney   Singapore

This book is a work of fiction. Names, characters, places and incidents are products of the author's imagination or are used fictitiously. Any resemblance to actual events or locales or persons, living or dead, is entirely coincidental.

An *Original* Publication of POCKET BOOKS

POCKET BOOKS, a division of Simon & Schuster, Inc.
1230 Avenue of the Americas, New York, NY 10020

ISBN: 0-671-78498-6

First Pocket Books printing December 2001

10 9 8 7 6 5 4 3 2 1

POCKET and colophon are registered trademarks of Simon & Schuster, Inc.

For information regarding special discounts for bulk purchases, please contact Simon & Schuster Special Sales at 1-800-456-6798 or business@simonandschuster.com

Cover art by Stephen Gardner

Printed in the U.S.A.

For Jay and Char, two faithful readers,
two total nuts.

The children of evil are surely insane.

—JUDITH MORIAE

Author's Note

Faithful readers of this series have probably already read this note, but please allow me to repeat myself: You may notice time and/or character discrepancies between the books and the games (or the books and the books, for that matter). With the games, comics, and novelizations being written, revised, and produced at different times and by different people, complete consistency is nearly impossible. I can only apologize on behalf of us all, and hope that in spite of chronological errors, you will continue to enjoy the mix of corporate zombies and hapless heroes that makes *Resident Evil* so much fun—to write, and, if I'm lucky, to read.

PROLOGUE

FACED WITH HIS IMMEDIATE DEATH, SUR-
rounded by the diseased and dying as pieces of flaming
helicopter rained down from the skies, all Rodrigo Juan
Raval could think about was the girl. That, and getting
the hell out of the way.

She'll die too—

—move!

He dove for cover behind an unmarked tombstone as
the small cemetery rumbled and shook. With a shattering metal sound of high impact, a massive chunk of
smoking 'copter crashed into the far corner of the yard,
spraying the nearest rotting prisoners and soldiers with
burning fuel. Bright, oily streamers of it spattered across
the ground like sticky lava—

—and when Rodrigo hit the dirt, he felt a tremendous
bolt of pain in his gut, two of his ribs cracking against a

weed-buried slab of dark marble. The pain was sudden and terrible, paralyzing, but he somehow managed not to pass out. He couldn't afford to.

A rotor blade knifed into the dirt barely two feet from him, spraying sandy earth into the evening sky. He heard a new chorus of wordless moans, the virus carriers protesting the rain of fire. An infected guard shambled by, his hair blazing like a torch, his eyes sightless and searching.

They don't feel it, don't feel a thing, Rodrigo desperately reminded himself, concentrating on his breathing, afraid to move as the pain edged from shrieking to mere shouting. *Not human anymore.*

The air was thick with dizzying fumes and the smells of rapid decay and burning meat. He heard a few gunshots somewhere else in the prison compound, but only a few; the battle was over, and they had all lost. Rodrigo closed his eyes for as long as he dared, fairly certain that he would never see another sunrise. Talk about having a crappy day.

It had all started only ten days before, in Paris. The Redfield girl had infiltrated HQ Admin, and had put up one hell of a vicious fight before Rodrigo himself had gotten the draw on her. The truth was, he'd been lucky—she'd pulled her piece and come up empty.

Yeah, real lucky, he thought bitterly. If he'd known what the immediate future was going to hold, he might have reloaded for her.

The reward for catching her alive, a chance to take his elite security unit through their paces with real, living viral carriers out at the Rockfort facility, the compound on a remote island in the Southern Atlantic. The girl would end up a new test subject for the scientists, or maybe bait for her troublesome brother and his hayseed S.T.A.R.S. rebellion Rodrigo kept hearing rumors about. Seventeen people had been seriously injured by Redfield's dance through HQ Admin, five more dead. Most of them were sleazy suits, Rodrigo hadn't given a half shit about any of them, but catching the girl meant he could look forward to a serious pay hike. Umbrella could turn her into a giant neon cockroach for all he cared, they'd certainly done worse.

Lucky again, it seemed. He had ten days to ready his troops, ten days while the HQ interrogators unsuccessfully questioned the girl. The journey from Paris to Capetown to Rockfort had been cake—the pilots were all top-notch and the girl had wisely kept her trap shut. All of his men had been psyched for the opportunity, the mood high as they touched down and started to prep for the first drills.

And then, less than eight hours after reaching the island—only the second time he'd ever been there—the compound had been brutally attacked by persons unknown, a precision air strike from out of the blue. Corporate financing, definitely, razor technology and seemingly unlimited supplies of ammo—the 'copters and planes had rolled overhead like a thundering black nightmare, the attack well-planned and merciless. As far as he could tell, everything was hit—the prison, the labs, the training facility. . . . He thought the Ashford house might have been spared, but he wouldn't bet on it.

The strike was devastating enough, but it was almost immediately trumped by what came next—the destroyed hot zone lab leaked out a half dozen variations on the T-virus, and a number of experimental BOWs, bio-organics, had escaped. The T series turned humans into brain-fried cannibals, an unfortunate side effect, but it hadn't been created for people. Through the questionable miracles of modern science, most of the new weapon subjects weren't even remotely human, and the virus turned them into killing machines.

Chaos had ensued. The base commander, that creepy maniac Alfred Ashford, hadn't done a damned thing to organize, so it had been up to the ranking soldiers to lead. The prisoners were obviously useless but there had been enough grunts on the ground to launch a tremendously unsuccessful defense and counterattack; his own boys had fallen as quickly as the rest of them, wiped out on their way to the heliport by a trio of OR1s, the current T-virus breed of choice.

All that training lost in just a minute or two. The OR1s were particularly nasty, violently aggressive and extremely powerful. Fortunately, only a few of those had escaped . . . but then, a few was all it took. Bandersnatches, the grunts called them, because of the long reach. Funny, that his team had been so careful to avoid infection, donning custom filter masks even as the first bombs hit—and yet they were taken out by a form of the virus, anyway.

At least it was over fast, before they even knew how much trouble they were in, he thought, envying them their hope. He hurt, he was exhausted, and he'd seen things that he knew would haunt him for the rest of his life, however long that might turn out to be. *They were the lucky ones.*

Rockfort had become a hell on Earth. The man-made

virus was a short-lived airborne and had dispersed quickly, only infecting about half the island's population . . . but the new carriers had promptly chomped down on most of the other half, spreading the disease. Some had escaped early on, but between the infected and the freed BOWs, getting out had become a bleak option. The entire island was overrun.

Maybe that's the way it should be. Maybe we all got what we deserved.

Rodrigo knew he wasn't an evil man, but he didn't kid himself, he wasn't exactly one of the good guys, either. He'd turned a blind eye to some very bad shit in exchange for some very good pay, and as much as he'd like to shift the blame around, he couldn't deny his own small part in the apocalypse that now surrounded him. Umbrella had been playing with fire . . . but even after Raccoon City had gone down, even after the disasters at Caliban Cove and the underground facility, he'd never really considered that something might happen to him or his team.

Another walking corpse wandered past his temporary shelter, a reasonably fresh shotgun blast where his jaw should have been. Rodrigo instinctively ducked lower and again had to struggle not to pass out, the fresh pain shockingly intense. He'd broken ribs before; this was something else, something internal. Liver laceration, maybe, a sure killer if he didn't get help. Assuming his amazingly bad lucky streak held up, he'd bleed out internally before something ate him . . .

His thoughts were wandering, the pain had gone deep and as much as he wanted to rest, there was the girl, he couldn't forget about her. He was close now, so close.

One of the guards had knocked her unconscious before she got her physical exam or prison issue, and that had been just before the attack. She should still be in the isolation cell, the underground entrance just past the flaming helicopter debris.

Almost finished now, then I can rest.

Most of the barely-human virus carriers had moved away from the fiery crash, following some primal instinct, perhaps. He'd lost his weapon somewhere along the way, but if he ran behind the standing headstones at the west wall . . .

Rodrigo eased himself into a sitting position, the pain getting worse, making him feel nauseous and weak. There should be a bottle of hemostatic liquid in the holding area's first aid kit, which would at least slow any internal hemorrhaging—although he thought he was prepared to accept death, as much as anyone could be prepared.

But not until I get to the girl. I captured her, I brought her here. My fault, and if I die, she dies, too.

In spite of all the horror he'd witnessed that day, the comrades he'd lost and the constant, gnawing terror of suffering a truly ghastly death, he couldn't stop thinking about her. Claire Redfield had blood on her hands, true, but not on purpose, not like Umbrella. Not like him. She hadn't killed for greed, she hadn't made him disregard his own conscience for all those years . . . and having watched his elite team turned into spaghetti by honest to God monsters, having spent the afternoon fighting for his life, it had become clear that trying to bring Umbrella to justice was what good guys did. The girl deserved something for that, even if only not to die alone

6

and in the dark. And it just so happened that he had a set of keys taken from the dead warden's belt loop, one of which would surely fit her cell door.

Sparks flurried up into the darkening sky from the flaming wreckage, tiny bright insects bursting into nothing, occasionally falling on one of the closer zombies and sizzling into their gray flesh before dying out. They didn't care. Rodrigo gritted his teeth and stumbled to his feet, aware that the young Claire probably wouldn't last ten minutes on her own, knowing that he meant to give her the chance. It wasn't the least he could do; it was simply the only thing left.

ONE

CLAIRE'S HEAD HURT.

She'd been half-dreaming, remembering things, until the faraway sound of thunder crowded through the dark, pulling her closer to wakefulness. She'd dreamed about the insanity that had become her life over the past few months, and even though an almost conscious part of her knew it was reality, it still seemed too incredible to be true. Flashes of what had happened in post-viral Raccoon City kept rising up, images of the inhuman creature that had stalked her and the little girl through the devastation, memories of the Birken family, of meeting Leon, of praying that Chris was all right.

Thunder again, louder, and she realized that something was wrong but couldn't seem to wake up, to stop remembering. Chris. Her brother had gone underground in Europe, and they had followed, and now she was cold and her head hurt but she didn't know why.

What happened? She concentrated, but it would only come in pieces, pictures and thoughts from the weeks since Raccoon City. She couldn't seem to control the memories. It was like watching a movie in a dream, and still, she couldn't wake up.

Images of Trent on the plane, and a desert, finding a disk of codes that had ultimately proved useless to her brother's cause. The long flight to London, the hop to France—

—a telephone call, "Chris is here, he's fine." Barry Burton's voice, deep and friendly. Laughing, the incredible relief filling her up, feeling Leon's hand on her shoulder—

It was a start, and it led her to the next clear recollection—a meeting had been set up, one of the surveillance posts for the HQ Admin wing, on Umbrella grounds. Leon and the others were waiting in the van, *checking my watch, heart pounding with excitement, where is he, where's Chris?*

Claire didn't know she was screwed until the first bullets ripped past, chasing her onto the spotlight-riddled grounds, into a building—

—running through the corridors, deafened by the rattle of automatic weapons and the helicopter outside, running, bullets chipping by close enough to send sharpened slivers of floor tile into the meat of her calves—

—and an explosion, armed soldiers writhing in the blast's fury, and . . . and I got caught.

They'd held her for over a week, trying everything

10

they could to make her talk. She'd talked, too, about going fishing with Chris, political ideology, her favorite bands. . . . When it came down to it, she didn't know anything vital; she was looking for her brother, that was all, and she somehow managed to convince them that she didn't know anything important about Umbrella. It probably helped that she was nineteen, and looked about as deadly as a Girl Scout. What little she actually *did* know, things about the Umbrella insider, Trent, or the whereabouts of Sherry Birken, the scientist's daughter, she buried deep and left there.

When they'd realized she was useless as an informant, she'd been taken away. Cuffed, scared, two private planes and a helicopter later, the island. She didn't even see it, they'd put a hood over her face, the stifling blackness only adding to her fear. Rockfort Island, wasn't that what the pilot called it? It was a long way from Paris, but that was the extent of her knowledge. Thunder, there was a sound of thunder. She remembered being pushed through a muddy prison cemetery in the gray morning, catching a glimpse through her stifling hood of the graves, marked with elaborate headstones. Down some stairs, welcome to your new home and BOOM—

The ground was shaking, rumbling. Claire opened her eyes just in time to see the one overhead light go out, the thick metal bars of her cell suddenly imprinted in negative and floating off to her left in the pitch dark. She lay on her side on a clammy, dirty floor.

Not good, nope, you better get up. Steeling herself against the pounding of her skull she crawled to her knees, her muscles stiff and sore. The blackness of the cold, dank room was very still, except for the sound of water dripping, a slow and lonely sound; it appeared she was alone.

Not for long. Oh, man, I'm in it deep now. Umbrella had her, and considering the havoc she'd created back in Paris, it was unlikely that they were going to treat her to ice cream and send her on her way.

The renewed awareness of her situation knotted her stomach, but she did her best to put the fear aside. She needed to think straight, to figure out her options, and she needed to be ready to act. She wouldn't have survived Raccoon City if she'd given in to panic—

—except you're on an island run *by Umbrella. Even if you get past the guards, where can you possibly go?*

One predicament at a time. First thing, she should probably try to stand up. Except for the painful lump at her right temple from the asshole who'd knocked her out, she didn't think she'd been injured—

There was another rumble, muffled and far away, and a bit of rock dust drifted down from above, she could feel it on the back of her neck. She had integrated the rumbling sounds into her half-conscious dreams as thunder, but it definitely sounded like heavy artillery had come to Rockfort. Or Godzilla. What the hell was going on out there?

She crept to her feet, wincing at her rifle-butt headache as she brushed dust off her bare arms, stretching chilled muscles. The underground room was making her wish she'd worn something warmer than jeans and a cut-off vest for her meeting with Chris—

—Chris! Oh, please be safe! In Paris, she'd deliberately led the Umbrella security team away from Leon

and the others, Rebecca and the two Exeter S.T.A.R.S.; if Chris hadn't also been caught, Claire figured he'd have hooked up with the team by now. If she could get to a computer with an uplink, she should be able to send a message to Leon . . .

. . . *yeah, just bend those steel bars, find a couple of machine guns, and mow down the population of the island. Oh, then hack into a tightly secured relay system, assuming you can find an unmanned computer. All so you can tell Leon that you don't actually know where Rockfort is—*

A louder internal voice cut in. —*think positive, damnit, you can be sarcastic later, assuming you survive. What do you have to work with?*

Good question. There was no guard, for one thing. It was also extremely dark, a bare hint of light coming from somewhere off to the right, which could be an advantage if—

Claire patted her pockets suddenly, wildly hoping that no one had searched her when she'd been unconscious, sure that someone must have—left inside vest pocket, there it was!

"Idiots," she whispered, pulling out the old metal lighter that Chris had given her awhile back, the comforting weight of it warm in her hand. When they'd patted her down for weapons, a soldier reeking of tobacco had taken it out, but given it back to her when she'd said that she smoked.

Claire put the lighter back in her pocket, not wanting to blind herself now that her eyes were getting used to the dark. There was enough ambient light for her to make out most of the small room—a desk and a couple of cabinets directly across from her cell, an open door to the left—the same door she'd entered by—a chair and some miscellaneous crap stacked off to the right.

Okay, good, you know the environment. What else you got?

Thankfully, her inner voice was a lot calmer than she was. She quickly went through her other pockets, turning up a couple of ponytail elastics and two breath mints in a crumpled roll. Terrific. Unless she wanted to take on the enemy with a very small, refreshingly peppermint slingshot, she was shit out of luck—

Footsteps, in the corridor outside the cell room, coming closer. Her muscles tensed and her mouth went dry. She was unarmed and trapped, and the way a few of those guards had been looking at her on the transport. . . .

. . . bring it on. I'm unarmed, maybe, but not defenseless. If someone meant to assault her, sexually or otherwise, she'd make a point of doing some major damage in return. If she was going to die anyway, she didn't plan on going out alone.

Thump. Thump. There was only one person out there, she decided, and whoever it was, he or she was hurting. The steps were erratic and slow, shuffling, almost like . . .

No, no way.

Claire held her breath as a lone male figure stepped haltingly into the room, his arms out in front of him. He moved like one of the virus zombies, like a drunk, reeling and unsteady, and immediately staggered for the door to her cell. Reflexively, Claire backed away, terrified at the implications—if there'd been some kind of viral outbreak on the island, at best she'd end up starving to death behind bars.

And Jesus, another *spill?* Thousands had died in Raccoon City. When would Umbrella learn, that their insane biological experiments weren't worth the cost?

She had to see. If it was a drunk guard, at least he was alone, she might be able to take him. And if it was a carrier, she was safe for the moment. Probably. They couldn't operate doors, or at least the ones in Raccoon hadn't been able to. She took out the lighter, flipped the top and thumbed the wheel.

Claire recognized him instantly and gasped, taking another step back. Tall and well-built, Hispanic perhaps, a mustache and dark, merciless eyes. It was the man who'd caught her back in Paris, who'd escorted her to the island.

Not a zombie, at least there's that. Not much of relief, but she'd take whatever she could get.

She stood for a moment, frozen, not sure what to expect. He looked different, and it was more than his dirt-smeared face or the small bloodstains on his white T-shirt. It was as though there'd been some fundamental internal change, the way his expression was set. Before, he'd looked like a stone killer. Now . . . now she wasn't sure, and when he reached into his pocket and pulled out a set of keys, she prayed that he'd changed for the better.

Without a word, he pulled the cell door open and blankly met her gaze before jerking his head to one side—the universal sign for "get out," if there was such a thing.

Before she could act, he turned and staggered away, definitely injured from the way he held his gut with one shaking hand. There was a chair between the desk and the far wall; he sat down heavily and picked up a small bottle from the desktop with bloodstained fingers. He shook the bottle, about the size of a small spool of thread, before weakly throwing it across the room, muttering to himself.

"Perfect . . ."

The presumably empty bottle clattered across the cement floor, rolling to a stop just outside the cell. He glanced in her direction tiredly, his voice thick with exhaustion. "Go on. Get out of here."

Claire took a step toward the open cell door and hesitated, wondering if it was some kind of trick—being shot trying to "escape" crossed her mind, and didn't seem all that far-fetched, considering who he worked for. She still clearly remembered the look in his eyes when he'd shoved that gun in her face, the cold sneer that had twisted his mouth.

She cleared her throat nervously, deciding to probe for an explanation. "What are you telling me, exactly?"

"You're free," he said, muttering to himself again as he sank deeper into the chair, chin lowering to his chest. "I don't know, might have been some kind of special forces team, troops were all wiped out . . . no chance of escape." He closed his eyes.

Her instincts told her that he really meant to let her go, but she wasn't going to take any chances. She stepped out of the cell and picked up the bottle he'd thrown, moving very slowly, watching him carefully as she approached. She didn't think his wounded act was a fake; he looked like hell, an ashy-white pallor over his dark skin, like a transparent mask. He wasn't breathing all that evenly, either, and his clothes smelled like sweat and chemical smoke.

She glanced at the bottle, an empty syringe vial with an unpronounceable name on the label, catching the word *hemostatic* in the fine print. Hemo was blood . . . some kind of bleeding stabilizer?

Maybe an internal injury . . . She wanted to ask him why he was releasing her, what the situation was outside, where she should go—but she could see that he was on the verge of passing out, his eyelids fluttering.

I can't just walk out, not without trying to help him——screw that! Go, go now!

He might die . . .

You *might die! Run for it!* The internal dispute was brief, but her conscience triumphed over reason, as usual. He obviously hadn't set her loose because of some personal affinity, but whatever the reason, she was grateful. He didn't have to let her go, and he'd done it anyway.

"What about you?" She asked, wondering if there was anything she *could* do for him. She certainly couldn't carry him out, and she was no medic—

"Don't worry about me," he said, raising his head to glare at her for a second, sounding irritated that she'd even brought it up.

Before she could ask him what had happened outside, he lost consciousness, his shoulders slumping, his body growing still. He was breathing, but without a doctor, she wouldn't want to bet on how long.

The lighter was getting hot, but she endured the heat long enough to search the small room, starting with the desk. There was a combat knife thrown casually on the blotter, a number of loose papers. . . . She saw her own name on one of them and scanned the document while fixing the knife sheath to her waistband.

Claire Redfield, prisoner number WKD4496, date of transfer, blah blah blah . . . escorted by Rodrigo Juan Raval, 3rd Security Unit CO, Umbrella Medical, Paris.

Rodrigo. The man who'd caught her and set her free, and now appeared to be dying right in front of her. She couldn't do anything about it, either, not unless she could find help.

Which I can't do down here, she thought, snapping the overheated lighter closed after she finished the rest of her search. Nothing but junk, mostly, a trunk of musty prisoner uniforms, endless stacks of paperwork stuffed into the desk. She'd found the pair of fingerless gloves they'd taken from her, her old riding gloves, and put them on, grateful for the minor warmth they provided. All she had to defend herself with was the combat knife, a deadly weapon in the right hands . . . which, unfortunately, hers weren't.

It's a gift horse, don't complain. Five minutes ago you were unarmed and locked up, at least now you have a chance. You should just be happy that Rodrigo didn't come down here to put you out of your misery.

Still, she pretty much sucked at knifeplay. After a brief hesitation, she quickly patted Rodrigo down, but he wasn't carrying. She did find a set of keys but didn't take them, not wanting to carry anything that might draw someone's attention by jangling at the wrong moment. If she needed them, she could come back.

Time to blow this Popsicle stand, see what there is to see out there.

"Let's do it," she said softly, as much to get herself moving as anything else, aware that she was basically terrified of what she might find . . . and also that she didn't have a choice in the matter. As long as she was on the island, Umbrella still had her—and until she assessed the circumstances, she couldn't make plans to escape.

Holding the knife tightly, Claire stepped out of the cellar room, wondering if Umbrella's madness would ever end.

Alone, Alfred Ashford sat on the wide, sweeping stairs of his home, half blind with rage. The destruction had finally ceased raining down from the skies, but his home had been damaged, *their* home. It had been built for his grandfather's great-grandmother—the brilliant and beautiful Veronica, God rest her soul—on the isolated oasis that she had named Rockfort, where she had made a magical life for herself and her progeny over the generations . . . and now, in the blink of an eye, some horrible fanatic group had dared to try and destroy it. Most of the second floor architecture had been warped and twisted, doors crushed shut, only their private rooms left whole.

Uncouth, uncultured miscreants. They can't even fathom the measure of their own ignorance.

Alexia was weeping upstairs, her delicate rose of a heart surely aching with the loss. The mere thought of his sister's needless pain fueled his rage to greater intensity, making him want to strike out—but there was no one to submit to his anger, all the commanding officers and chief scientists dead, even his own personal staff. He'd watched it happen from the safety of the private mansion's secret monitor room, each tiny screen telling a different story of brutal suffering and pathetic incompetence. Almost everyone had died, and the rest had run like frightened rabbits; most of the island's planes were already gone. His personal cook had been the only survivor in the common receiving mansion, but she'd screamed so much that he himself had been forced to shoot her.

We're still here, though, safe from the unwashed hands of the world. The Ashfords will survive and prosper, to dance on the graves of our adversaries, to drink champagne from the skulls of their children.

He imagined dancing with Alexia, holding her close, waltzing to the dynamic music of their enemies' tortured screams. . . . It would be nothing short of bliss, his twin's gaze locked to his, sharing the awareness of their superiority over the common man, over the stupidity of those who sought to destroy them.

The question was, who had been responsible for the attack? Umbrella had many enemies, from legitimate rival pharmaceutical companies to private shareholders—the loss of Raccoon City had been disastrous for the market—to the few closet competitors of White Umbrella, their covert bioweapons research department. Umbrella Pharmaceutical, the brainchild of Lord Oswell Spencer and Alfred's own grandfather, Edward Ashford, was extremely lucrative, an industrial empire . . . but the real power lay with Umbrella's clandestine activities, the operations of which had become too vast to remain entirely unnoticed. And there were spies everywhere.

Alfred clenched his fists, frustrated, his entire body a live wire of furious tension—and was suddenly aware of Alexia's presence behind him, a trace of gardenia in the air. He'd been so intent on his emotional chaos that he hadn't even heard her approach.

"You mustn't let yourself despair, my brother," she said gently, and stepped down to sit beside him. "We will prevail; we always have."

She knew him so well. When she'd been away from Rockfort all those years ago, he'd been so lonely, so afraid that they might lose some of their special connection . . . but if anything, they were closer now than ever before. They never spoke about their separation, about the things that had happened after the experiments at the Antarctic facility, both of them just so happy to be together that they would say nothing to spoil it. She felt the same way, he was certain.

He gazed at her for long seconds, soothed by her graceful presence, astounded as always by the depths of her beauty. If he hadn't heard her weeping in her bedroom, he wouldn't have known that she'd shed a tear. Her porcelain skin was radiant, her sky-blue eyes clear and shining. Even today, this darkest of days, the very sight of her gave him such pleasure . . .

"What would I do without you?" Alfred asked softly, knowing that the answer was too painful to consider. He'd gone half-mad with loneliness when she'd been away, and sometimes still had strange episodes, nightmares that he was alone, that Alexia had left him. It was one of the reasons he encouraged her never to leave their heavily secured private residence, located behind the visitor mansion. She didn't mind; she had her studies, and was aware that she was too important, too exquisite to be admired by just anyone, quite content to be sustained by her brother's affections, trusting him to be her sole contact with the outside world.

If only I could stay with her all the time, just the two of us, hidden away... But no, he was an Ashford, responsible for the Ashford's stake in Umbrella, accountable for the entire Rockfort compound. When their basically incompetent father, Alexander Ashford, had gone missing some fifteen years before, the young Alfred had stepped up to take his place. The key players behind Umbrella's bioweapons research had tried to keep him out of the loop, but only because he intimidated them, cowed them by the natural supremacy of his family name. Now they sent him regular reports, respectfully explaining the decisions they made on his behalf, making it clear that they would get in touch with him immediately if the need arose.

I suppose I should contact them, tell them what's happened. . . . He'd always left those matters to his personal secretary, Robert Dorson, but Robert had left his service some weeks before to join the other prisoners, after expressing a bit too much curiosity about Alexia.

She was smiling at him now, her face glowing with understanding and adoration. Yes, she was so much better to him since her return to Rockfort, truly as devoted to him as he'd always been to her.

"You'll protect me, won't you," she said, not a question. "You'll find out who did this to us, and then show them what one gets for trying to destroy a legacy as powerful as ours."

Overcome with love, Alfred reached out to touch her but stopped short, all too aware that she didn't like physical contact. He nodded instead, some of his rage returning as he thought of someone trying to harm his beloved Alexia. Never, not as long as he lived, would he allow that to happen.

"Yes, Alexia," he said passionately. "I'll make them suffer, I swear it."

He could see in her eyes that she believed in him, and his heart filled with pride, just as his thoughts turned to the discovery of their enemy. An absolute hatred for Rockfort's assailants was growing inside of him, for the stain of weakness they had tried to paint on the Ashford name.

I'll teach them regret, Alexia, and they'll never forget the lesson.

His sister relied on him. Alfred would die before letting her down.

Two

CLAIRE SNAPPED THE LIGHTER CLOSED AT the base of the covered stairs and took a deep breath, trying to psych herself up for whatever came next. The chill of the dark corridor behind her pressed at her back like an icy hand, but still she hesitated, the knife haft sweaty beneath her fingers as she slipped the warm lighter into her vest pocket. She wasn't particularly looking forward to ascending into the unknown, but she had nowhere else to go, not unless she meant to go back to the cell. She could smell oily smoke, and she guessed that the flickering shadows at the top of the wide cement steps meant fire.

But what's up there? This is *an Umbrella facility . . .* What if it was like Raccoon City, what if the attack on the island had unleashed a virus, or some of the animal abominations that Umbrella kept creating? Or was Rockfort only a prison for their enemies? Maybe the prisoners had rioted, maybe things had only been bad from Rodrigo's point of view . . .

. . . maybe you could walk up the goddamn stairs and find out instead of guessing all day, hmm?

Her pulse thumping, Claire forced herself to take the first step up, vaguely wondering why movies always made it seem so easy, to bravely throw oneself into probable danger. After Raccoon, she knew better. Maybe she didn't have much of a choice about what she had to do, but that didn't mean she wasn't scared. Considering the circumstances, only a complete moron wouldn't be afraid.

She climbed slowly, opening her senses as new adrenaline flushed her system, replaying the brief glimpse she'd had of the small graveyard when the guards had led her through. No help there, she'd only seen a few headstones, remembered them as bizarrely ornate for a prison cemetery. There was definitely a fire close to the top of the stairs, but apparently not a big one—there was no heat filtering down, only a cool and humid breeze that carried the pervasive smoke smell. It seemed quiet, and as she neared the top, she heard drops of rain hissing as they met the flames, an oddly comforting sound.

As she emerged from the stairwell, she saw the source of the fire, only meters away. A helicopter had crashed, a large portion of it merrily burning amid a thick, smoking haze. To her left was a wall, another just past the flaming wreck; to her right, the open space of the cemetery, gloomy and shrouded by the increasing rain and the oncoming night.

Claire squinted into the rainy dusk and made out a number of dark shapes, though none of them seemed to be moving; more headstones, she thought. A whisper of relief edged through her anxiety; whatever had happened seemed to be over.

Amazing, she thought, that she could possibly be relieved to be alone in a cemetery at night. Even six months ago, her imagination would have conjured up all sorts of horrible things. It appeared that ghosts and cursed souls just didn't cut it on the scary meter anymore, not after her run-ins with Umbrella.

She took a right on the U-shaped path, moving slowly, remembering how she'd been led through the graveyard before being pushed to the stairs. She thought she could make out what looked like a gate past the line of graves in the center of the yard, or at least an open space in the far wall—

—and suddenly she was flying, the sound of an explosion behind her assaulting her ears, WHUMP, a wave of broiling heat throwing her into the mud. The wet twilight was suddenly brighter, the reek of burning chemicals stinging her nose and eyes. She landed without grace but managed not to stab herself with the combat knife, all of it happening so fast that she barely had time to register confusion.

—don't think I'm hurt—helicopter's fuel tank must have blown—

"Unnnh . . ."

Claire was on her feet instantly, the soft, pitiful, unmistakable moan inspiring a near panic of action, the sound joined by another, and another. She spun around and saw the first one stumbling toward her from what was left of the burning helicopter, a man, his clothes and hair on fire, the skin of his face blistering and black.

She turned again and saw two more of them crawling up from the mud, their faces a sickening gray-white, their skeletal fingers grasping in her direction, clutching air as they reeled toward her.

Shit! Just as in Raccoon, Umbrella's viral synthesis had effectively turned them into zombies, stealing their humanity and their lives.

She didn't have time for disbelief or dismay, not with three of them closing in, not when she realized that there were others farther along the path. They staggered out from the shadows, slack, brutalized faces all turning slowly toward her, mouths hanging open, their gazes blank and unchanging. Some wore shreds of uniforms, camo or plain gray, guards and prisoners. There had been a spill, after all.

"Uhhhh . . ."

"Ohhh . . ."

The overlapping cries epitomized great longing, each plaintive wail that of a starving man looking at a feast. Goddamn Umbrella for what they'd done! It was beyond tragic, the transformation from human into mindless, dying creatures, decaying as they walked. The inevitable fate of each virus carrier was death, but she couldn't let herself mourn for them, not now, her pity limited by the need to survive.

Go go go NOW!

Her assessment and analysis lasted less than a second and then she was moving, no plan except to get away. With the path blocked in both directions, she leaped for the center of the graveyard, clambering over the marble slabs that marked the resting places of the true dead. Her wet, muddy jeans clung to her legs, hampering her, her boots slipping against the smooth headstones, but she managed to climb up and balance her weight between two of them, out of reach for the moment.

For the second! *You gotta get out of here, fast.* The knife was no good, she didn't dare get close enough to use it—a single healthy bite from one of those things and she'd end up joining their ranks, if they didn't eat her first.

The one with the blackened face was nearest, his hair melted away, part of his shirt still smoldering. He was close enough for her to smell the greasy, nauseating smell of burnt flesh, overlaid by the stench of the fuel that had cooked it. She had ten, fifteen seconds at most before he'd be close enough to grab for her.

She shot a glance at the southeast corner of the yard, her arms out for balance. There were only two of them between her and the exit, but that was two too many, she'd never make it past both of them. She knew from Raccoon that they were slow, and that their reasoning skills were zip—they saw prey, they moved toward it in a straight line, regardless of what was in the way. If she could just bait them away from the gate—

Good idea, except there were too many on the ground, six or seven of them, she'd end up surrounded—

—*but not if you stay on the headstones.*

There were multiple zombies to either side of the center row of graves, but only one standing at the end of the line, directly in front of her . . . and that one barely functional, an eye gouged out, an arm broken and hanging.

It was a risky plan, one stumble and she was toast, but the burned man was already reaching for her ankle with his charred and shaking hands, rain sizzling on his upturned face.

Claire leaped, arms wheeling as she landed with both feet on the narrow top of the next stone slab in line. She started to pitch forward, jerking and swiveling her body to maintain her center of gravity, but it was no good, she was going to fall—

—and without thinking, she quickly jumped again, then again, using the uneven stones like rocks in a river, using her lack of balance to propel her forward. An ashen-faced virus carrier snatched at her lower legs, moaning in feverish hunger, but she was already past it, leaping to the next headstone. She didn't have time to consider how she was going to stop, which was just as well—because the unlikely path ran out one jump later and her next leap was into a sloppy shoulder roll against the muddy ground a meter below.

Oof, a hard drop, but she followed through and came up on her feet, just barely, her legs sliding unsteadily in the muck. The one-eyed zombie lurched toward her, gurgling, within easy reach—but she quickly stumbled around it, keeping on its blind side, the knife ready. The creature attempted to turn, to find its meal once more, but she easily stayed out of its limited sight.

She risked a glance away from her awkward, shuffling dance and saw the other zombies closing in. The rain intensified, sluicing the mud off of her.

It's working, just another few seconds—

Frustrated by its lack of success, the half-blinded carrier pawed at the air with its one good arm. The dirty, blackened nails scraped across her chest and the zombie moaned anxiously, scrabbling at the wet denim, but it couldn't get a solid grip.

God, it's touching me—

With a wordless cry of fear and disgust Claire slashed out with the knife, deep, nearly bloodless cuts opening up across its wrist. The zombie continued to clutch at her, oblivious to the damage she was doing as it staggered closer, and Claire decided that it was time to leave.

She pulled her arms back, hands fisted, and then drove them forward into the creature's chest, pushing as hard as she could. She turned again to the center line of graves as the creature fell backward, the others much closer now.

How she managed to climb back up so quickly she didn't know; one second she was on the ground, the next she was on top of beveled granite. She saw that the exit was clear, the zombies now loosely grouped near the west wall.

Her hopping second journey along the headstones was only slightly more controlled than the first, each leap like a leap of faith, that she wouldn't slip and seriously injure herself. The rain was tapering off, and she could hear the wet, sucking sounds of their plodding, slow-motion chase clearly; unless one of them suddenly remembered how to jog, they were too far away to catch up to her.

Now I just have to pray that the door isn't secured, she thought dizzily, jumping down from the last headstone. The gate was standing open, but the door just past it wasn't; if it turned out to be locked, she was probably doomed.

Three giant strides from where she landed, she was through the gate and reaching for the handle of a dented metal door, the exit set into the stone wall. It clicked open smoothly and she held the knife ready, hoping that if there were more carriers on the other side, at least the odds might be better. Behind her, the chemical cannibals lamented their loss, moaning loudly as she stepped through.

Some kind of courtyard, piled with pieces of random wreckage, overlooked by a low guard tower. There was an overturned transport vehicle to her left, a low fire burning inside. The night was coming on quickly but the moon was also rising, either full or close to it, and as she secured the door behind her, she could see there was no immediate danger—no zombies headed toward her, anyway. There were several bodies strewn about, none of them moving, and she mentally crossed her fingers that at least one of them had a gun and some ammo—

A brilliant light suddenly snapped on, a spotlight on the guard tower, the force of it instantly blinding her—

—and as she instinctively looked away, the whining chatter of automatic fire broke out, bullets splashing in the mud at her feet. Blind and panicked, Claire dove for cover, the random thought that she might have been better off in that cell repeating itself through her terror.

The fighting had been over for some time, the last gunshots maybe an hour past, but Steve Burnside thought he might stay where he was for a while, just in case. Besides, it was still raining a little, a bitter ocean wind picking up. The guard tower was safe and dry, no dead people and no zombies wandering around, and he'd be able to see anyone coming in plenty of time to head them off . . . with a little help from the machine gun mounted on the window ledge, of course, a seriously kick-ass weapon. He'd mowed down all the courtyard zombies without breaking a sweat. He had a handgun, too, a 9mm semi that he'd taken off one of the past-tense guards, which also kicked ass, though not quite as much.

So, hang here another hour or so, assuming it doesn't start pouring again, then go find a way off this rock.

He thought he could handle a plane, he'd seen his . . . he'd been in cockpits often enough, but he thought a boat might be better—not as far to fall if he screwed the pooch, so to speak.

Steve leaned casually against the cement window ledge, looking out over the moonlit courtyard, wondering if he should try to find a kitchen before ditching out. The guards hadn't gotten around to serving lunch, being as how they were all dying, and it seemed they didn't stock the tower room with doughnuts or whatever, he'd already looked. He was starving.

Maybe I should head for Europe, get myself some international cuisine. I can go anywhere I want now, anywhere at all. There's nothing holding me back.

The thought was supposed to get him excited for all the possibilities, but it didn't, it made him feel anxious and kind of weird, so he went back to considering his escape. The main gate that led out of the prison was locked down, but he figured if he searched enough guards, he'd find one of the emblem keys. He'd already run across the warden, the late Paul Steiner, but all his keys were gone.

So was most of his face, Steve thought, not particularly unhappy about it. Steiner had been a serious dick, strutting around like he was King Turd of Shit Mountain, always smiling when another prisoner got led off to the infirmary. And nobody ever came back from the infirmary—

—*snick.*

Steve froze, staring at the metal door straight across from the tower. The graveyard was on the other side, and he knew for a fact it was full of zombies, he'd sneaked a look right after plugging the courtyard corpses. Jesus, could they open doors? They were walking vegetables, mush brains, they weren't supposed to be able to open *doors,* and if they could do that, what else were they capable of—

—*don't panic. You've got the machine gun, remember?*

All of the other prisoners were dead. If it was a person, he or she was no friend of his . . . and if it wasn't human, or was a zombie, he'd be putting it out of its misery. Either way, he wasn't going to hesitate, and he wasn't going to be afraid. Fear was for pussies.

Steve grabbed for the searchlight handle with his right hand, his left already on the trigger guard of the heavy black rifle. As the door swung open, he swallowed dryly and snapped the light on, firing as soon as he had the target pinned down.

The weapon rattled out a stream of bullets, the handle jouncing against his hand, rounds kicking up tiny fountains of mud. He caught a glimpse of something pink, a shirt maybe, and then his target was diving out of the line of fire, moving way too fast to be one of the cannibals. He'd heard about some of the monsters Umbrella had cooked up and machine gun or no, he hoped to God he wasn't about to meet one of them.

I'm not afraid, I'm not—He tracked right with the searchlight and kept firing, a sudden anxious sweat on his brow. The person or thing was behind the protruding wall near the base of the tower, out of sight, but if he couldn't kill it, he could at least scare it away. Cement chips flew, the high-intensity beam illuminating the lower half of a dead prison guard, mud, and debris, but no target—

—and there was a lightning flash of motion from behind the wall, a glimpse of pale, upturned face—

BAM! BAM! BAM!

—and the searchlight shattered, white-hot chunks of glass spraying across the tower room floor. Steve let out an involuntary yell as he jumped back from the machine gun, somebody was *shooting* at him, and he didn't care if it was pussy, he was about to shit his pants.

"Don't shoot!" he shouted, his voice breaking. "I give!"

It was dead silent for a few seconds, and then a cool female voice came out of the dark, low and somehow amused.

"Say Uncle."

Steve blinked uncertainly, confused—and then remembered how to breathe again, feeling his cheeks go red as the fear fell away.

"I give," that was totally lame. So much for first impressions.

"I'm coming down," he said, relieved that his voice didn't break this time, deciding that anyone who could make a joke after being shot at couldn't be all bad. If she was the enemy, he had the 9mm . . . but friendly or not, there was no way he was going to ask her not to shoot again, that would just make him look worse.

And it's a girl . . . maybe a pretty one . . .

He did his best to ignore the thought, no point in getting his hopes up. For all he knew, she was ninety-eight, bald, and smoked cigars . . . but even if she wasn't, even if she was a total hottie, he didn't want to end up taking responsibility for any life besides his own, screw that shit. He was free now. Having someone count on you was almost as bad as having to depend on others . . . .

The thought was uncomfortable, and he pushed it aside. Anyway, the circumstances weren't exactly romantic, what with a bunch of diseased monsters running wild and death around every corner. Gross, slimy death, too, the kind with maggots and pus.

Steve took the steps to the courtyard two at a time, his eyes adjusting to the post-searchlight dark as he stepped out to meet her. She stood in the center of the courtyard, a gun in hand . . . and as he got closer, it was all he could do not to stare.

She was muddy and wet and about the most beautiful girl he'd ever seen, her face like a model's, big eyes and fine, even features. Reddish hair in a dripping ponytail. An inch or two shorter than him, and about the same age, he thought—he'd be eighteen in a couple of months, and she couldn't be much older. She wore jeans, boots, and a sleeveless pink vest over a tight black half tee, her flat stomach showing, the entire outfit accentuating her lean, athletic body . . . and although she looked tired and wary, her gray-blue eyes sparkled brightly.

Say something cool, play it cool no matter what. . . .

Steve wanted to tell her he was sorry about firing at her, to tell her who he was and what had happened during the attack, to say something suave and worldly and interesting—

"You're not a zombie," he blurted, inwardly cursing even as it came out. Brilliant.

"No shit," she said mildly, and he suddenly realized that her weapon was pointing *at* him, she held it low, but she was definitely aiming it. Even as he froze she took a step back and raised the gun, watching him closely, her finger under the trigger guard and the muzzle only inches from his face. "And who the hell are you?"

The kid smiled. If he was nervous, he was doing a good job of not letting it show. Claire didn't take her finger off the trigger, but she was already half convinced that he was no threat to her. She'd shot out the light, but he easily could have strafed the yard and taken her down.

"Relax, beautiful," he said, still smiling. "My name's Steve Burnside, I'm—I *was* a prisoner here."

"Beautiful?" Oh, great. Nothing annoyed her more than being patronized. On the other hand, he was obviously younger than her, which probably meant he was just trying to assert his maleness, to be a man rather than a boy. In her experience, there were few things more ob-

noxious than someone trying to be something they weren't.

He looked her up and down, obviously checking her out, and she took another step back, the gun unwavering; she wasn't going to take any chances. The weapon was an M93R, an Italian 9mm, an excellent handgun and apparently standard issue for the prison guards; Chris had one of them. She'd found it after diving for cover, next to the dead, outstretched fingers of a man in uniform . . . and if she shot the young Mr. Burnside with it at this range, most of his handsome face would be on the ground. He looked like an actor she'd seen before, the lead in that movie about the sinking ship; the resemblance was striking.

"I'm guessing you're not from Umbrella, either," he said casually. "I'm sorry about opening up on you like that, by the way. I didn't think there was anyone else alive around here, so when the door opened . . . " He shrugged.

"Anyway," he said, cocking an eyebrow, obviously trying to be charming. "What's your name?"

There was no way Umbrella had hired this kid, she was more sure of it with each word out of his mouth. She slowly lowered the semiautomatic, wondering why Umbrella would want to imprison someone so young.

They wanted to imprison you, remember? She was only nineteen.

"Claire, Claire Redfield," she said. "I was brought here as a prisoner just today."

"Talk about timing," Steve said, and she had to smile a little at that; she'd been thinking the same thing herself.

"Claire, that's a nice name," he continued, looking into her eyes. "I'll definitely remember that."

Oh, brother. She wondered if she should shut him down now or later—she and Leon had gotten pretty tight—and decided that later might be better. There was no question that she'd have to take him with her to look for an escape, and she didn't want to deal with his reproach along the way.

"Well, much as I'd like to hang around, I've got a plane to catch," he said, sighing melodramatically. "Assuming I can find one. I'll look for you before I take off. Be careful, this place is dangerous."

He started toward a door next to the guard tower, directly opposite from the one she'd come through. "Catch you later."

She was so surprised that she almost couldn't find her voice in time. Was he nuts, or just stupid? He was at the door before she spoke up, jogging after him.

"Steve, wait! We should stick together—"

He turned and shook his head, his expression incredibly condescending. "I don't want you following me, okay? No offense, but you'll just slow me down."

He smiled winningly again, working the eye contact as hard as he could. "And you'd *definitely* be a distraction. Look, just keep your eyes and ears open, you'll be fine."

He was through the door and gone before she could say anything. Dumbfounded and thoroughly annoyed, she watched the door settle closed, wondering how he had survived so far. His attitude suggested that he thought this was just one big video game, where he couldn't possibly get hurt or killed. It appeared that sheer bravado counted for something . . . the one thing teenaged boys seemed to have in abundance.

That and testosterone.

If being perceived as cool was his main concern, he wasn't going to make it very far. She had to go after him, she couldn't leave him to die—

Arroooooooo . . .

The terrible, lonely, ferocious sound that suddenly shattered the still night was one she'd heard before, in Raccoon City, and it was coming from behind the door that Steve had just gone through. There was no mistaking it for anything else. A dog, infected by the T-virus, turned from a domestic animal into a ruthless killer.

After a fast search of the dead guards in the courtyard, she had two more full clips and part of a third. As ready as she was going to get, Claire took a few deep breaths and then slowly pushed the door open with the 9mm's barrel, hoping that Steve Burnside would stay lucky until she found him . . . and that by meeting him, her own luck hadn't just taken a serious turn for the worse.

THREE

AS TERRIBLE AND DISHEARTENING AS THE DE-struction to Rockfort, Alfred couldn't deny that he enjoyed putting down a few of his subordinates on the way to the training facility's main control room. He'd had no idea how gratifying it could be to see them sick and dying, reaching for him in hunger—the same men who'd sneered at him behind his back, who'd called him abnormal, who had pretended allegiance with their fingers crossed—and then expiring by his hand. There were listening devices and hidden cameras throughout the compound, installed by his own paranoid father, a hidden monitor room in the private residence; Alfred had known all along that he wasn't liked, that the Umbrella employees feared but didn't respect him as he deserved.

And now . . .

Now it didn't matter, he thought, smiling, stepping

out of the elevator to see John Barton at the other end of the hall, staggering toward him with outstretched arms. Barton had been responsible for training Umbrella's growing militia in small arms, at least at the Rockfort compound, and had been a loud, vulgar barbarian— swaggering around with his cheap cigars, flexing his ridiculously bloated muscles, always sweating, always laughing. The pale, blood-drenched creature stumbling toward him bore little resemblance, but was undoubtedly the same man.

"You're not laughing anymore, Mr. Barton," Alfred said lightly, raising his .22 rifle, using the sight to put a tiny red dot over the trainer's bloodshot left eye. The drooling, moaning Barton didn't notice—

Bam!

—although he surely would have appreciated Alfred's excellent aim and choice of ammunition. The .22 was loaded with safety slugs, rounds designed to spread out on impact—designated "safe" because the bullet wouldn't go through the target and injure anyone else. Alfred's shot obliterated Barton's eye and certainly a goodly part of his brain, rendering him harmless and quite dead. The large man crumpled to the floor, a puddle of blood spreading out beneath him.

Some of the BOWs were unnerving to him, and he was relieved that most had either been locked down in various parts of the training facility or had been killed outright—he certainly wouldn't be wandering around if there were more than a few on the loose—but he didn't find the virus carriers to be particularly frightening. Alfred had seen many men—and a number of women, as well—turned into these zombie-like creatures by way of the T-virus, experiments that he'd witnessed throughout his childhood, that he'd directed himself as an adult. In fact, there were never more than fifty or sixty prisoners living at Rockfort at a time; between Dr. Stoker, the anatomist and researcher who'd worked at the "infirmary," and the constant need for training targets and spare parts, no one incarcerated at the compound enjoyed Umbrella's hospitality for more than six months.

And where will we all be six months from now, I wonder?

Alfred stepped over Barton's swollen corpse, walking toward the control room to call his Umbrella HQ contacts. Would Umbrella choose to rebuild at Rockfort? Would he agree to it? He and Alexia had been perfectly safe from the virus during its "hot" stage, both pathways between the rest of the facility and their private home locked down throughout most of the air attack, but knowing that Umbrella's nameless enemy was willing to resort to such extreme measures, did he really want to risk refitting a laboratory so near their home? The Ashfords feared nothing, but neither were they reckless.

Alexia would never agree to closing the facility, not now, not when she's so close to her goal. . . .

Alfred stopped in his tracks, staring at the banks of radio and video equipment, at the blank computer screens that stared back at him with wide dead eyes. He stared but didn't see, a strange emptiness opening up inside of him, confusing him. Where was Alexia? What goal?

Gone. She's gone.

It was true, he could feel it in his bones—but how

could she leave him, how could she when she knew that she was his heart, that he would die without her?

The monstrosity, screaming and blind, a failure and it was cold, so cold, the queen ant naked, suspended in the sea and he couldn't touch her, could only feel the cold unyielding glass beneath his longing fingers—

Alfred gasped, the nightmare imagery so real, so horrid that he didn't know where he was, didn't know what he was doing. Distantly, he felt his hands clenching tighter and tighter around something, the muscles of his arms shaking—

—and there was a burst of static from the console in front of him, loud and crackling, and Alfred realized that somebody was speaking.

". . . please, if anyone can hear me—this is Doctor Mario Tica, in the second floor lab," the voice was saying, breaking with fear. "I'm locked in, and all the tanks have gone down, they're waking up—please, you have to help me, I'm not infected, I'm in a suit, swear to God, you gotta get me out of here—"

Dr. Tica, locked in the embryo tank room. Tica, who had long been sending private reports to Umbrella about his progress with the Albinoid project, secret reports that were different than the ones he showed Alfred. Alexia had suggested that Tica be sent to Dr. Stoker some months ago . . . wouldn't she be amused, to hear him now?

Alfred reached over and turned off Tica's babbling plea, suddenly feeling much better. Alexia had warned him time and again about his peculiar episodes, the flashes of intense loneliness and confusion—stress, she insisted, telling him that he was not to take them seriously, that she would never leave him voluntarily. She loved him too much for that.

Thinking of her, thinking of all the trouble and pain that Umbrella's incompetent defenses had brought about for them both, Alfred abruptly decided not to place his uplink call. HQ had certainly heard about the attack by now, and would be sending a cleanup crew soon enough; really, there was no need to speak with them . . . and besides, they didn't deserve to hear his observations of the situation, to have foreknowledge of the dangers they'd be facing. He was no employee, no ignorant lackey who had to report to his superiors. The Ashfords had created Umbrella; they should be reporting to *him*.

And I did speak to Jackson only a week ago, about the Redfield girl—

Alfred felt his eyes widen, his mind working madly. Claire Redfield, sister to Chris Redfield, he of the meddlesome S.T.A.R.S. holdouts, had arrived mere hours before the attack. She had been caught in Paris, inside Umbrella's HQ Administration building, claiming to be searching for her brother—and they'd sent her to him, to keep her locked up while they decided what to do with her.

But . . . what if the plan had been to lure her brother out into the open, to crush his ridiculous insurrection once and for all, a plan they'd conveniently forgotten to tell him? And what if she'd been followed to Rockfort by Redfield and his comrades, her very presence a signal for them to attack . . .

. . . or perhaps even allowed herself to be captured in the first place?

It was as if a puzzle was falling into place. Of course,

of course she had. Clever girl, she'd played her part well. Whether or not Umbrella had unwittingly encouraged the attack didn't matter, not now, he would deal with them later; what mattered was that the Redfield witch had brought the enemy to Rockfort, and she might still be alive, stealing information, spying, perhaps even planning to, to *hurt* his Alexia—

"No," he breathed, the fear immediately transforming into fury. Obviously that had been her plan all along, to do as much damage to Umbrella as possible—and Alexia was undoubtedly the brightest scientific mind working in bioweapons research, perhaps the brightest in any field.

Claire wouldn't get away with it. He'd find her . . . or, better yet, wait for her to come to him, as she surely would. He could watch for her, lay in wait like a hunter, the girl his prey.

And why kill her immediately, when you could have so much fun with her first? It was Alexia's voice in his thoughts, reminding him of their childhood games, the pleasure they'd shared in their own experiments, creating environments of pain, watching things suffer and die. It had forged the bond between them in steel, to share such intimate things. . . .

. . . I can keep her alive, let Alexia play with her . . . or better, I could invent a maze for her, see how she fares against some of our pets. . . . There were many possibilities. With few exceptions, Alfred could unlock all the doors on the island by computer; he could easily lead her wherever he wanted, and kill her at his discretion.

Claire Redfield had underestimated him, they all had,

but no more . . . and if things worked out the way Alfred was starting to hope, the day would end on a much happier note than the dismal discord which had marked its beginning.

If there were infected dogs roaming the grounds, they were hiding. The open yard Claire stepped into was littered with corpses, their flesh a sickly gray beneath the pale moonlight except for where the countless splashes of blood had fallen; no dogs, nothing moving except the low clouds scudding across the thickening night sky. Claire stood for a moment, watching the shadows, wanting to make sure of her surroundings before leaving the exit behind.

"Steve," she whispered harshly, afraid to shout for fear of what might be lurking. Unfortunately, Steve Burnside was as scarce as the howling dog she'd heard; he hadn't just wandered away, it seemed, he'd taken off at a sprint.

Why? Why would he choose to be alone? Maybe she was wrong, but Steve's bit about not wanting to be slowed down just didn't ring true. When she'd unknowingly stumbled into the Raccoon nightmare, running into Leon had made all the difference in the world; they hadn't stuck together the entire time, but just knowing that there was someone else as shocked and scared as she was . . . instead of feeling helpless and isolated, she'd been able to form clear objectives, goals beyond mere survival—finding transportation out of the city, looking for Chris, taking care of Sherry Birken.

And simply from a safety standpoint, having someone

to watch your back is a hell of a lot better than going it solo, no question.

Whatever his reason, she was going to do her damnedest to talk him out of it, assuming she could find him. The yard in front of her was much bigger than the one she'd just stepped out of, a long, one-story cabin to her right, a wall without doors to her left, the back of a larger building, perhaps. A low fire was burning in one of the wall's broken windows, and there was plenty of debris strewn among the dead, evidence of the force-ful attack. To her immediate right was a locked gate, a moonlit dirt path on the other side, and a closed door . . . which meant that Steve was either in the cabin or had gone around it, using the trail at the far end of the yard that also headed to the right.

She decided to try the cabin first . . . and as she hopped the few steps up to the railed porch that ran most of the length of the building, she found herself wonder-ing who had attacked Rockfort, and why. Rodrigo had said something about a special forces team, but if that was true, whose orders were they following? It seemed that Umbrella had its share of enemies, which was defi-nitely good news—but the island attack was a tragedy nonetheless. Prisoners had died along with employees, and the T-virus—perhaps the G-virus, too, and God only know how many others—didn't differentiate between the guilty and the innocent.

She had reached the plain wooden door of the cabin, and holding the 9mm at the ready, she gently pushed it open—and immediately closed it, her course decided by the two virus carriers she'd seen inside, both stumbling around a table. A second later there was a *thump* at the door, a low, pitiful moan filtering out.

The trail it is, then. She doubted that the cocksure Steve would have left anyone standing had he gone into the cabin, and she probably would have heard the shots—

—unless they got him first.

Claire didn't like it, but the grim reality of her situation was that she couldn't afford to waste the ammo to find out. She'd follow the path, see where that led ... and if she couldn't find him then, he was on his own. She wanted to do the right thing, but she also felt pretty strongly about saving her own ass; she had to get back to Paris, to Chris and the others, which she certainly couldn't do if she blew her ammo and ended up being someone's lunch.

She moved back along the porch, all of her senses on high as she neared the end of the building. She hadn't forgotten about the zombie dog or dogs, and listened for the patter of claws against dirt, for the heavy panting that she remembered from her previous experience in Raccoon. The damp, chill night was quiet, a shivering breeze sweeping lightly through the yard, the only breathing she heard her own.

A quick glance around the corner of the cabin; nothing, only a man's body lying half in and half out of the building's crawl space, some five meters away. Another ten past that and the path turned right again, much to Claire's relief—she'd seen that leg of the trail through the locked gate, and it had been empty then.

So he must have gone through that door, the one on the west wall ... It was also a relief to know something, to know *anything* certain when it came to Umbrella. She started down the path, thinking about what it would take to convince the macho teen to stay with her. Maybe if she told him about Raccoon, explained that she'd had some practice with Umbrella disasters . . .

Claire was just about to step over the lone corpse's upper body when it moved.

She jumped back, her semi pointed at the man's bloody head, her heart hammering—and she realized that he *was* dead, that someone or something in the shadows of the crawl space was pulling him inside by his legs, a strong and steady series of jerks—

—like a dog backing up with something heavy in its jaws.

She didn't think anything after that, instinctively leaping over the dead man and sprinting away, aware that the dog—if that's what it was—wouldn't be preoccupied forever. The realization that it had been less than a meter away lent her speed as she took the corner, her boots slapping against the wet, hard packed earth, her arms pumping. Zombies were slow, uncoordinated; the dogs that both she and Leon had run across were vicious and lightning quick. Even armed, she wasn't interested in facing off with one of them, a single bite and she'd be infected, too.

Arrrooooo! The gurgling howl came from farther away than the crawl space, from somewhere back in the front part of the yard.

Shit, how many— Didn't matter, she was almost there, her salvation ahead on the left. Not daring to look back, she didn't slow down a step until she reached the door, grabbed the handle and shoved. It opened easily, and since she didn't see anything with teeth directly in front of her, she jumped in and slammed the door behind her—

—only to hear the multiple wails of zombies, to smell the feverish rot of the dying virus carriers even as something crashed into the door at her back and began to claw at it, growling like some feral monster.

How many dogs, how many zombies? The thought flashed through her panicked mind, the need to conserve ammo deeply ingrained after Raccoon, *and what if I'm about to hit a dead end?* She almost turned back in spite of the risk, until she saw where the zombies were.

The passage she'd entered was thick with gloom, but she could see several stumbling men locked in a caged area to her left, all of them pretty far gone. One of them was beating on the mesh door, its nearly skeletal hands hanging with ribbons of damaged tissue, oblivious to the pain of its disintegrating body.

Must be the kennel . . .

Claire took a few steps farther in, focusing worriedly on the simple and somewhat flimsy lock holding the door closed—and saw the three uncaged zombies just as the first was reaching for her, its gaping mouth dripping with saliva and some other dark fluid, its bony fingers stretching out to touch her. She'd been so intent on the caged creatures, she hadn't realized that there were more of them.

She reflexively dropped her weight and snapped her left leg into its chest, a solid and effective side kick that knocked the creature back. She could feel her boot sink into its deteriorating flesh but didn't have time for disgust, already bringing the 9mm up—

—and with a thin metallic *crash*, the kennel door banged open, and suddenly she was facing seven instead of three. They crowded toward her, clumsily maneuvering past a Dumpster, a few barrels, the bodies of their fallen brethren.

Bam! She shot the closest one without thinking, a neat hole punching through its right temple, understanding that she was doomed as it crumpled and hit the dirt. Too many, too tightly grouped, she'd never make it—

—*the barrels!* One of them was marked flammable, *same trick I used in Paris*—

Claire dove for cover behind the Dumpster, switching the gun to her left hand as she landed. The target marked in her mind's eye, she came up shooting, only her arm curling around the Dumpster as the confused zombies teetered and searched, moaning hungrily—

Bam! Bam! B—

—*KA-BLAM!*

The Dumpster slammed into her right shoulder, knocking her over backward. She curled into a ball on her side, ears ringing, as jagged, burning shreds of metal rained down from above, clattering atop the Dumpster, a few of them landing on her left leg. She slapped them off, scarcely able to believe that it had worked, that she was still alive.

She sat up, pushing herself into a crouch, looking out at what remained of her assailants. Only one of them was still whole, leaning heavily on the kennel, its clothes and hair on fire; the upper body of a second was trying to crawl toward her, its black and bubbling skin sloughing off as it inched forward. The rest were in pieces, the burning earth licking up to claim the pathetic remains as its own.

Claire quickly dispatched the two left alive, her heart aching a little at the dismal end these people had come to. Ever since Raccoon City, her dreams were haunted by zombies, by the stinking, dripping creatures that sought live flesh as sustenance. Umbrella had unintentionally created these particular monsters, like nightmarish walking corpses straight out of the movies, and it was kill or be killed, there was no choice.

Except they were people *not so long ago.* People with families and lives, who hadn't deserved to die in such terrible ways, no matter what evils they may have committed. She looked down at the poor burned bodies, feeling almost sick with pity—and a low but insistent fever of hatred for Umbrella.

Claire shook her head and did her best to let it go, aware that allowing herself to carry all that pain might make her hesitate at some crucial moment. Like a soldier at war, she couldn't afford to humanize the enemy . . . although she had no doubts as to who the real enemy was, and she hoped fervently that Umbrella's leaders would all burn in hell for what they'd done.

Not wanting to be surprised again, she carefully and thoroughly checked the passage's shadows in her evaluation of next-step choices. In the back of the kennel was an actual guillotine, stained with what appeared to be real blood. Just looking at it made her shudder, reminding her of RPD's Chief Irons, and his hidden dungeon; Irons had been living proof that Umbrella didn't run psych tests on their undercover employees. Behind the nasty execution device was a door, but Steve obviously hadn't gone that way, not with the zombies locked in. Next to the kennel was a kind of metal sliding shutter, but it wouldn't open . . . and next to that, the only door he could have gone through, because the passage was a dead end just past it.

Claire walked to the door, suddenly feeling very tired and very old, her emotions spent. She checked the handgun and then reached for the handle, absently wondering if she would ever see her brother again. Sometimes holding on to her hope was a tremendous burden, made all the heavier because she couldn't set it aside, not even for a moment.

Steve jumped when he heard the explosion outside, reflexively looking around at the small, cluttered office as though expecting the walls to crumble. After a few beats he relaxed, figuring it was probably just another heat blast, nothing to worry about. Ever since the attack, the unchecked fires burning throughout the prison compound occasionally rolled over something combustible, a canister of oxygen or kerosene or whatever, and then *ker-blooey*, another explosion.

It was just such a blast that had kept him alive, actually—he'd been knocked out by a flying chunk of wall when an oil barrel had blown up, the debris covering him completely, hiding him. When he'd finally come to, the big zombie chow-down was pretty much over, most of the prison guards and prisoners already dead. . . .

Bad train of thought. He shook it off and returned his attention to the computer screen, to the file directory he'd stumbled across while trying to find a map of the island. Some dumbass had written the pass code number on a sticky note and slapped it on the hard drive, giving him easy access to some obviously secret stuff. Too bad most of it was dull as dishwater—prison budgeting, names and dates he didn't recognize, information about some kind of special alloy that metal detectors couldn't pick up . . . that one was kind of interesting, considering he'd had to walk through a two-way lockdown metal detector to get to the office, but three or four well-placed bullets to the mechanism had taken care of *that*. Good thing, too; he'd found one of the main gate emblem keys tucked in a desk drawer, which would definitely have triggered a lockdown on his way back through.

All I need is a goddamn map to the nearest boat or plane and I'm history. He'd pick up the chick after he cleared a path, too, play the knight in shining armor . . . and she'd undoubtedly be appreciative, maybe even enough to want to—

A name on the file directory caught his eye. Steve frowned, peering closer at the screen. There was a folder labeled *Redfield, C.* . . . as in Claire Redfield? He tapped it up, curious, and was still reading, totally absorbed, when he heard a noise behind him.

He scooped his gun off the counter and spun around, mentally kicking himself for not paying better attention—and there was Claire, her own weapon pointing at the floor, a slightly irritated look on her face.

"What are you doing?" she asked casually, as if she hadn't just scared the crap out of him. "And how did you get past the zombies outside?"

"I ran," he answered, annoyed by the question. Did she think he was helpless or something? "And I'm looking for a map . . . hey, are you related to a Christopher Redfield?"

Claire frowned. "Chris is my brother. Why?"

Siblings. That explains it. Steve motioned toward the computer, vaguely wondering if the entire Redfield clan kicked ass. Her brother sure as hell did, ex-Air Force pilot and S.T.A.R.S. team member, a competition marksman and a serious thorn in Umbrella's side. No way he would have admitted it out loud, but Steve was kind of impressed.

"You might want to tell him that Umbrella's got him under surveillance," he said, stepping back so she could read what was on the screen. Apparently Redfield was in Paris, though Umbrella hadn't managed to locate his exact whereabouts. Steve was glad that he'd run across a file that meant something to her; a little gratitude from a pretty girl was always a good thing.

Claire scanned the info and then tapped a few keys, glancing back at him with a look of relief. "Thank God for private satellites. I can get through to Leon, he's a friend, he should have hooked up with Chris by now. . . ."

She'd already started typing, absently explaining herself as her fingers moved across the keys. ". . . there's a message board we both use . . . there, see? 'Contact ASAP, the gang's all here.' He posted the night I was caught."

Steve shrugged, not really interested in the life and times of Claire's pals. "Go back a file, the longitude and latitude of this rock are written down," he said, smiling a little. "Why don't you send your brother directions, let him come save the day?"

He expected another irritated look, but Claire only nodded, her expression dead serious. "Good idea. I'll say there's been a spill at these coordinates. They'll know what I mean."

She was pretty, all right, but also pretty naive. "That was a *joke*," he said, shaking his head. They were in the middle of nowhere.

She was staring at him. "Hilarious. I'll tell it to Chris when he shows up."

Entirely without warning, a fiery rage welled up inside of him, a tornado of anger and despair and a whole bunch of feelings he couldn't even begin to understand. What he *did* understand was that little Miss Claire was wrong, she was stupid and snotty and wrong.

"Are you kidding? You actually expect him to show, with what's going on here? And look at the coordinates!" The words came out hot and fast and louder than he intended, but he didn't care. "Don't be such an idiot—believe me, you can't depend on people like that, you'll only get hurt in the end, and then you'll have nobody to blame but yourself!"

Now she was looking at him like he'd lost his mind, and on top of his fury came a crushing wave of shame, that he'd freak out for no good reason. He could feel tears threatening, only adding to his humiliation, and there was no way he was going to cry in front of her like some baby, no way. Before she could say anything, he turned and ran, blushing furiously.

"Steve, wait!"

He slammed the office door behind him and kept going, wanting only to get out, to get away, *hell with the map, I've got the key, I'll figure something out and I'll kill anything that tries to stop me—*

Through the long hall, past the dead metal detector and out, his weapon ready, a part of him bitterly disappointed as he ran past the kennel, twice nearly tripping over wet and smoldering body parts—there was nothing to shoot, no one to blast into oblivion, to make him stop feeling whatever it was he was feeling.

He barreled through the door that came out behind the bunkhouse and started around the long building, sweating, his heart pounding, his thick hair sticking to his scalp in spite of the cold air—and he was so focused on his own strange madness, his need to run, that he didn't see or hear anything coming until it was almost too late.

Wham, something hit him from behind, knocking him sprawling. Steve immediately rolled onto his back, a sudden mortal terror blocking out everything else—and there were two of them, two of the prison's guard dogs, one of them circling back from having jumped on him, the other growling deep in its throat, its legs stiff and head down as it slowly approached.

Jesus, look at 'em—

They had been rottweilers, but not anymore; they'd been infected, he could see it in their glazed red eyes and dripping muzzles, in the strange new ridges of muscle that flexed and bunched beneath their almost slimy-looking coats. And for the first time since the attack, the immensity of Umbrella's craziness—their secret experiments, their ridiculous cloak and dagger mentality—really hit home. Steve liked dogs, a hell of a lot more than he liked most people, and what had happened to these two poor animals wasn't fair.

Not fair, wrong place at the wrong time, I didn't deserve any of this, I didn't do anything wrong—

He wasn't even aware that the object of his pity had changed, that he was admitting to himself how shitty things really were, how badly he'd been screwed; he didn't have time to notice. It had been less than a second since he'd rolled onto his back, and the dogs were getting ready to attack.

It was over in another second, the time it took to pull the trigger once, pivot, pull it again. Both animals went down instantly, the first taking it in the head, the second, in the chest. The second dog let out a single *yip* of pain or fear or surprise before it collapsed in the mud, and Steve's hatred for Umbrella multiplied exponentially with that strangled sound, his mind repeating again and again how unfair it all was as he crawled to his feet and broke into a stumbling run. He had the key to the prison gate; he wasn't going to be their captive anymore.

Time for a little payback, he thought grimly, suddenly hoping, *praying* that he crossed paths with one of them, one of the sick, decision-making asshole bastards who worked for Umbrella. Maybe if he got to hear them beg for death, maybe then he'd feel a little better.

FOUR

CHRIS REDFIELD AND BARRY BURTON WERE reloading rounds in the back room of the Paris safe house, silent and tense, neither of them speaking. It had been a bad ten days, not knowing what had happened to Claire, not knowing if Umbrella still had her alive. . . .

. . . *stop,* his inner voice said firmly. *She's alive, she has to be.* To even entertain the alternative was unthinkable.

He'd been telling himself that for ten days, and it was wearing thin. It had been bad enough hearing that she'd been in Raccoon City for the final meltdown, and that she'd gone there looking for him. Leon Kennedy, her young cop friend, had filled him in on the details at their first meeting. She'd survived Raccoon only to be hijacked by Trent on the way to Europe, she and Leon and the three renegade S.T.A.R.S.; they'd ended up facing off with yet another group of Umbrella monsters, at a facility in Utah. Chris hadn't known about any of it, had ignorantly assumed that she was still safely studying away at the University.

Hearing that she'd gotten tangled up in the fight against Umbrella was bad, all right—but knowing that Umbrella had captured her, that his little sister might already be dead . . . it was killing him, eating him up inside. It was all he could do not to barge into Umbrella's headquarters with a couple of machine guns and start demanding answers, even knowing that it would be suicide.

Barry pumped the shell loader while Chris scooped up the fresh rounds and boxed them, the acrid, familiar scent of gunpowder suffusing the air. He was relieved that his old friend seemed to understand his need for silence, the steady *click-click* of the loader the only sound in the small room.

It was also a relief to have something to do after a full week of sitting still and praying, hoping that Trent might contact them with news, or to offer help. Chris had never met Trent, but the mysterious stranger had aided the S.T.A.R.S. a few times in the past, passing along inside information about Umbrella. Although his exact motivations were unknown, his objective seemed clear enough—to destroy the pharmaceutical company's secret bioweapons division. Unfortunately, waiting on Trent was a long shot; he'd only ever contacted them when it suited his needs, and since they had no way of reaching him, the prospect of his assistance was seeming less likely all the time.

Click-click. Click-click. The repetitive sound was soothing somehow, a muted mechanical process in the quiet of the rented safe house. They all had specific jobs to do in their pledge to bring Umbrella down, tasks that changed from day to day as the need arose. Chris had been helping Barry out with the weapons for the past week and a half, but he usually ran HQ surveillance. They'd received a message from Jill a few weeks before, she was on her way to Paris, and Chris knew that her misspent youth would come in very handy for internal recon. Leon had turned out to be a half decent hacker, he was in the next room on the computer; he'd hardly slept since Claire's capture, most of his time spent trying to track Umbrella's recent movements. And the trio of S.T.A.R.S. who'd come with Claire and Leon to Europe—Rebecca, from the disbanded Raccoon squad, and the two S.T.A.R.S. from Maine, David and John— were currently off in London, meeting with an arms dealer. After all they'd been through together, the three of them worked well as a team.

There aren't many of us, but we've got the skills and the determination. Claire, though . . .

With both their parents dead, he and Claire had developed a close relationship, and he thought he knew her pretty well; she was smart and tough and resourceful, always had been . . . but she was also a college student, for Christ's sake. Unlike the rest of them, she didn't have any formal combat training. He couldn't help thinking that she'd been lucky so far, and when it came to Umbrella, luck just wasn't enough.

"Chris, get in here!"

Leon, and it sounded urgent. Chris and Barry looked at each other, Chris seeing his own worry mirrored in Barry's face, and they both stood up. His heart in his throat, Chris hurriedly led the way down the hall to where Leon was working, feeling eager and afraid at once.

The young cop was standing next to the computer, his expression unreadable.

"She's alive," Leon said simply.

Chris hadn't even been aware of how bad things had been for him until those two words. It was like his heart had suddenly been released after being gripped in a vise for ten days, the sense of relief as physical as it was emotional, his skin flushing with it.

Alive, she's alive—

Barry clapped him on the shoulder, laughing. "Of course she is, she's a Redfield."

Chris grinned, turned his attention back to Leon— and felt his smile slipping at the cop's carefully neutral expression. There was something else.

Before he could ask, Leon motioned at the screen, taking a deep breath. "They've got her on an island, Chris . . . and there's been an accident."

Chris was leaning over the computer in a single stride. He read the brief message twice, the reality of it slow to sink in.

Infection trouble approximately 37S, 12W following attack, perps unknown. No bad guys left, I think, but stuck at the moment. Watch your back, bro, they know the city if not the street. Will try to be home soon.

Chris stood up, silently locking gazes with Leon as Barry read the message. Leon smiled, but it looked forced.

"You didn't see her in Raccoon," he said. "She knows

how to handle herself, Chris. And she managed to get to a computer, right?"

Barry straightened up, took his cue from Leon. "That means she's not locked down," he said seriously. "And if Umbrella's got its hands full with another viral spill, they're not going to be paying attention to anything else. The important thing is that she's alive."

Chris nodded absently, mind already working on what he would need for the trip. The coordinates she'd listed put her in an incredibly isolated spot, deep in the South Atlantic, but he had an old Air Force buddy who owed him, could jet him down to Buenos Aires, maybe Capetown; he could rent a boat from there, *survival gear, rope, medkit, an assload of firepower* . . .

"I'm going with you," Barry said, accurately reading his expression. They'd been friends a long time.

"Me, too," Leon said.

Chris shook his head. "No, absolutely not."

Both men started to protest, and Chris raised his voice, talking over them.

"You saw what she said, about Umbrella honing in on me, on us," he said firmly. "That means we have to relocate, maybe one of the estates outside the city—someone has to stay here, wait for Rebecca's team to get back, and someone else needs to scout out a new base of operations. And don't forget, Jill will be here any day now."

Barry frowned, scratched at his beard, his mouth set in a thin, tight line. "I don't like it. Going in alone is a bad idea . . ."

"We're at a crucial phase right now, and you know it," Chris said. "Somebody's got to mind the shop, Barry, and you're the man. You've got the experience, you know all the contacts."

"Fine, but at least take the kid," Barry said, gesturing toward Leon. For once, Leon didn't protest the label, only nodded, drawing himself up, shoulders back and head high.

"If you won't do it for yourself, think about Claire," Barry continued. "What happens to her if you get yourself killed? You need a backup, somebody to pick up the ball if you fumble."

Chris shook his head, immovable. "You know better, Barry, this has to be as quiet as possible. Umbrella may have already sent in a cleanup crew. One person, in and out before anyone even realizes I'm there."

Barry was still frowning, but he didn't push it. Neither did Leon, although Chris could see that he was working up to it; the cop and Claire had obviously gotten pretty close.

"I'll bring her back," Chris said, softening his tone, looking at Leon. Leon hesitated, then nodded, high color burning in his cheeks, making Chris wonder exactly how close Leon and his sister had become.

Later. I can worry about his intentions if we make it back alive—

— when *we make it back alive,* he quickly amended. "If" was not an option.

"It's settled, then," Chris said. "Leon, find me a good map of the area, geographical, political, everything, you never know what might help. Also post back to Claire, just in case she gets another chance to check for messages—tell her I'm on my way. Barry, I want to be packing major influence, but lightweight, something I can hike in without too much trouble, maybe a Glock ... you're the expert, you decide."

Both men nodded, turned away to get started, and Chris closed his eyes for just a second, quickly offering up a silent prayer.

Please, please *stay safe until I get there, Claire.*

It wasn't much—but then, Chris had the feeling he would be praying a lot more in the long hours to come.

The hidden monitor room was behind a wall of books in the Ashfords' private residence. Upon his return to their home, secreted behind the "official" receiving mansion, Alfred slung his rifle and immediately walked to the wall, touching the spines of three books in quick succession. He felt a hundred pairs of eyes observing him from the front hall shadows, and though he had long since grown used to Alexia's scattered collection of dolls, he often wished that they wouldn't always watch him so intently. There were times that he expected some privacy.

As the wall pivoted open, he heard the whistling chitter of bats hiding in the eaves and frowned, pursing his lips. It seemed that the attic had been breached during the attack.

No mind, no mind. Concerns for another day. He had more important business that demanded his attention.

Alexia had apparently retreated to her rooms once more, which was just as well; Alfred didn't want her upset any further, and news of a possible assassin at Rockfort would certainly achieve that. He stepped inside the hidden room and pushed the carefully balanced wall closed behind him.

There were usually seventy-five different camera shots that he could choose from, to watch on any of the ten small monitors in the small room—but much of the equipment around the compound had been damaged or destroyed, leaving him with only thirty-one usable images. Knowing Claire's foul objectives, to steal information and search for Alexia, Alfred decided to focus on her approach from the prison compound. He had no doubt that she would appear shortly; one such as her would not have the good manners to die in the attack or its aftermath . . . though as his expectations built, his interest in the game growing, he began to feel anxious that she might, in fact, have expired.

Thankfully, his initial assumption had been correct. Another of the prisoners came through the main gate first, but he was followed shortly by the Redfield girl. Amused at their halting progress, Alfred watched as Claire tried to catch up to the young man, prisoner 267 according to the back of his uniform, who seemingly had no idea that he was being pursued.

As the young man topped the stairs that led up from the prison area, stood uncertainly looking between the palace grounds and the training facility, Alfred entered 267 into the keypad beneath his left hand and found a name, Steven Burnside. It meant nothing to him, and as the boy hesitated indecisively, Alfred found his attention moving back to his quarry, curious about the young woman who was soon to be his short-term playmate.

Claire was walking across the damaged chasm bridge only a moment or two behind Burnside, walking high on the balls of her feet like an athlete. She seemed quite self-possessed, cautious but unapologetic about her right to cross the span . . . but she was also careful not to look down into the mist-filled darkness, the massive crevice walls extending down hundreds of feet, nor did she linger. In the warm security of his home, Alfred smiled, imagining her delicious fear . . . and found himself remembering the trick that he and Alexia had once played on a guard.

They'd been six or seven years old, and Francois Celaux had been a shift commander, one of their father's favorites. He'd been a fawning sycophant, a bootlick, but only to Alexander Ashford. Behind their father's back he had dared to laugh cruelly at Alexia one afternoon when she had tripped in a pouring rain, splashing her new blue dress with mud. Such an offense was not to be withstood.

Oh, how we planned, talking late into the night about a suitable punishment for his unforgivable behavior, our child minds alive and whirling with all the possibilities . . .

The final plan had been simple, and they'd executed it perfectly only two days later, when Francois had duty as guard of the main gate. Alfred had sweetly begged the cook to let him bring Francois his morning espresso, a chore he'd often performed for favored employees . . . and on the way to the chasm bridge, Alexia had added a special twist to the strong, bitter brew, just a few drops of a curare-like substance she'd synthesized herself. The drug paralyzed flesh but allowed the nervous system to continue working, so that the recipient couldn't move or speak, but could feel and understand what was happening to him.

Alfred had approached the prison gates slowly, so

slowly that the impatient Francois had stalked out to meet him. Smiling, aware that Alexia had returned to the residence, was watching and listening from the monitor room—Alfred had been wearing a small microphone— he'd stepped close to the railing before apologetically offering the demitasse cup to Francois. Both twins had watched in secret delight as the guard swilled it down, and in seconds, he was gasping for air, leaning heavily against the bridge rail. To anyone watching, it appeared only that the man and boy were looking out across the chasm . . . except for Alexia, of course, who later told him that she'd applauded his performance of innocence.

I looked up at him, at the frozen expression of fear on his unrefined features, and explained what we had done. And what we were going to do.

Francois had actually managed a soft squealing noise through his clenched jaw when he'd finally understood, that he was helpless to defend himself against a child. For almost five minutes, Alfred had cheerfully cursed Francois as the spawn of pigs, as a mannerless peasant, and had jabbed him in the meat of his thigh with a sewing needle too many times to count.

Paralyzed, Francois Celaux could only endure the pain and humiliation, surely regretting his beastly con- duct toward Alexia as he suffered in silence. And when Alfred had tired of their game, he'd kicked the guard's dirty bootheels a few times, describing his every sensa- tion to Alexia as Francois slid helplessly beneath the rail and plummeted to his death.

And then I screamed, and pretended to cry as others came rushing across the bridge, trying desperately to console their young master as they asked one another how such a terrible thing could happen. And later, much later, Alexia came into my room and kissed my cheek, her lips warm and soft, her silken tresses tickling my throat—

The monitors tore his attention away from his sweet memories, Claire now standing at the same spot where Burnside had hesitated. Quite put out with himself for his lack of care, Alfred spent an uncertain moment searching for the young hoodlum, switching between cameras, finally spotting him on the very steps of the receiving mansion. Quickly, Alfred checked his console's control panels to be sure that all of the mansion's doors were unlocked, suspecting that the boy would probably hang himself easily enough—

—and crowed with delight when he saw that Claire was following, having chosen the same path as her young friend.

How much more exquisite her terror will be, when she pleads for her life kneeling in Mr. Burnside's cooling blood . . .

If he meant to greet them properly, he needed to leave right away. Alfred stood and opened the wall once more, his excitement rising as he closed it behind him and stepped out into the great hall. He very much wanted to tell Alexia his plans before leaving, to share a few of his ideas, but was concerned that time was a factor—

"I'll be watching, my dear," she said.

Startled, Alfred looked up to see her at the top of the stairs, not far from the life-size child doll that hung from the uppermost balcony, one of Alexia's favorite toys. He started to ask her how she knew, but realized how silly a question it was. Of course she knew, because she knew his heart; it was the same that beat within her own snowy white breast.

"Go now, Alfred," she said, gracing him with her smile. "Enjoy them for both of us."

"I will, sister," he said, smiling in turn, thankful anew that he was brother to such a miracle of creation, lucky that she so understood his needs and desires.

It was like some bizarre reality twist, Claire decided, closing the mansion doors behind her. From the ramshackle, death-filled cold of the dark prison yards to where she stood now . . . it was hard to believe, and yet so like Umbrella that she had no choice.

But goddamn. I mean, seriously.

The grand, beautifully designed sunken lobby spread out in front of her was marred only by a few sets of muddy footprints across the hand-tiled floor, a few splotches of blood painted across the delicate eggshell walls. There were also a number of large cracks near the ceiling, and a single maroon handprint drying on one of the thick decorative columns that lined the west wall, thin rivulets of red streaking down from the base of the palm.

So the prisoners weren't the only ones to suffer a shitty afternoon. It was classist and petty of her, she knew, but it made her feel a little better to know that the Umbrella higher-ups had taken an ass-kicking along with everybody else.

She stood where she was for a moment, relieved to be

out of the cold and still mildly shocked by the different faces of the Rockfort facility as she took in the layout. Behind one of the columns to her left was a blue door, a second door in the northwest corner of the spacious room. Straight ahead was a polished mahogany reception desk, abutting an open flight of stairs along the right wall that led up to a second floor balcony, richly hung with a strangely damaged portrait. The face of the portrait's subject had been scratched out for some reason.

Claire stepped down into the lobby, crouched and ran a finger through one of the muddy footprints; still wet, and more tracks leading to the corner door. She couldn't be certain they were Steve's, but thought the odds were pretty good. He'd left a trail, from the open prison gate to a couple of dropped shell casings just outside the mansion, along with two more dead dogs. For such an obviously troubled young man, he was a surprisingly accurate shot . . .

. . . so why am I going through so much trouble to help him out? She thought sourly, standing. *He doesn't want my assistance, doesn't seem to need it, and it's not like I don't have anything better to do.*

When he'd taken off running, she hadn't followed immediately, wanting to get a message to Leon ASAP; she'd also felt obliged to run a quick search of the office for medical supplies, something to help Rodrigo, but she hadn't found anything useful—

"Help! Help meee!" A muffled shout, from somewhere in the building.

Steve?

"Let me out! Hey, somebody, help!"

71

Claire was already running for the corner door, weapon up. She slammed into the heavy wood, the door crashing open into a long hallway. Steve shouted again, from the far end of the corridor. Claire hesitated just long enough to see that the three bodies sprawled on the tiled floor weren't going to get up and then ran, fixing the door straight ahead as the one.

"Help!"

Jesus, what's happening to him? He sounded panic-stricken, his voice breaking with it.

Reaching the end of the hall, Claire shoved at the door, ran in sweeping with the handgun—and saw nothing, a room with display cases and stuffed chairs. An alarm was buzzing somewhere, but she didn't see its source.

Movement to the left. Claire spun, desperate for a target—and saw that a piece of film was being projected on a small wall screen, silent and flickering. Two attractive blond children, a boy and girl, staring intently into each other's eyes. The boy was holding something, something wriggling—

—a dragonfly, and he's—

Claire looked away involuntarily, disgusted. The boy was pulling the wings off of the struggling insect, smiling, both of them smiling.

"Steve!" Why wasn't he shouting anymore, where was he? She had the wrong room, must be—

"Claire? Claire, in here! Open the door!"

His voice was coming from behind the projection screen. Claire dashed across the room, searching the wall, absently aware that the towheaded children had dropped the tortured dragonfly into a container full of ants, were watching the crippled bug being stung to death.

"What door, where?" Claire shouted, running anxious hands over the wall, pushing at a glass display case, pulling at the screen—

—and the screen raised up, disappearing into a slot. Behind it was a console, a keyboard, and six picture boxes in two rows of three, a switch beneath each one.

"Claire, do something, I'm burning up!"

"What do I do, how did you get in there? Steve!"

No answer, and she could hear the rising desperation in her voice, could feel it eating into her brain—

—*concentrate. Do it, now.*

Claire clamped down on her near panic, the clear voice in her mind the voice of intellect. If she panicked, Steve would die.

There's no door. There's a console with boxes.

Yes, that was it, that was the key. Steve yelled out another terrified plea, but Claire only looked at the boxes, focusing, *each is different, a boat, an ant, a gun, a knife, a gun, an airplane—*

They weren't all different, there were *two* guns, a semiautomatic handgun and a revolver, the switches labeled "C" and "E." Nothing else matched, and her first thought was that it was like one of those grade-school tests, which two are alike. Without questioning her reasoning, Claire reached out and flipped the two switches, the two boxes lighting up—

—and to her right, a display case slid out from the wall. The buzzing alarm stopped, and a blast of dry, baking heat expelled from the opening, washing over her. A half second later, Steve stumbled out and dropped to his knees, his arms and face beet red. He was holding a pair of matching handguns, what looked like gilded Lugers.

Guess I picked the right boxes.

She leaned over him, trying to remember what the signs of heatstroke were—dizziness and nausea, she thought. "Are you okay?"

Steve gazed up at her. With his flushed cheeks and vaguely embarrassed expression, he resembled nothing so much as a little boy who'd had too much sun. Then he grinned, and the illusion was lost.

"What took you so long?" he cracked, pushing himself to his feet.

Claire straightened, scowling. "You're welcome."

His grin softened and he ducked his head, pushing thick bangs away from his forehead. "Sorry . . . and I'm sorry about before, too. Thanks, seriously."

Claire sighed. Just when she'd decided he was a total asshole, *he* decided to be nice.

"And look what I got," he said, snapping both handguns up and aiming at one of the display cases. "They were hanging on a wall back there, fully loaded and everything. Cool, huh?"

She had to resist a sudden urge to grab his shoulders and shake some sense into him. He had nerve, she'd give him that, and he obviously had at least a *few* survival skills . . . but did he not understand that he would have died, if she hadn't heard him calling for help?

This place is probably full of booby traps, too; how do I keep him from running off again?

She watched him pretend-shoot a bookshelf, wondered absently if the whole macho thing was just his way of dealing with fear—and a different approach suddenly occurred to her, one that she thought might actually work.

He wants to play Mr. Tough Guy, let him. Appeal to his ego.

"Steve, I understand that you're not looking for a partner, but I am," she said, doing her best to look sincere. "I . . . I don't want to be alone out there."

She could actually see his chest puff out, and felt a huge sense of relief, knowing that it had worked before he said a word. She also felt a little guilty for manipulating him, but only a little; this was for the best.

Besides, it's not lying, exactly. I really don't *want to be alone out there.*

"I guess you could tag along," he said expansively. "I mean, if you're scared."

She only smiled, teeth gritted, aware that if she opened her mouth to thank him, she didn't know what would come out.

"And anyway, I know how to get us out of here," he added, his bluff manner slipping, his youthful enthusiasm spilling out. "There's a little map under the counter at the front desk. According to that, there's a dock just west of here, *and* an airstrip somewhere past that. Which means we have a choice, but my piloting skills are a little iffy, so I vote cruise. We can go right now."

Maybe she *had* underestimated him a bit. "Really? Great, that's . . . " Claire trailed off. Rodrigo, she couldn't forget about Rodrigo, *between the two of us we could probably get him to the dock . . .*

"Would you come with me back to the prison, first?" She asked. "The guy who let me out of my cell is back there, he's pretty badly wounded—"

"One of the prisoners?" Steve asked, perking up.

Uh-oh. She could lie, but he'd know the truth soon enough. "Um, I don't think so . . . but he *did* let me go, and I kinda feel like I owe him—"

Steve was frowning, and she quickly added, "—and it seems like the, uh, *honorable* thing to do, to at least get him a first-aid kit, you know?"

He wasn't buying. "Forget it. If he's not a prisoner, he works for Umbrella, he deserves dick. Besides, they'll be sending troops in soon enough; it's their problem, let them deal with it. Now, are you coming or not?"

Claire met his gaze squarely, reading anger and hurt in his dark eyes, surely caused by Umbrella. She couldn't blame him for how he felt, but she didn't agree with him, either, not in Rodrigo's case. And there was no question in her mind that he would die before Umbrella showed if he didn't get help.

"I guess not," she said.

Steve turned away, took a few steps toward the door and then stopped, sighing heavily. He turned back, clearly exasperated. "There's no way I'm risking my neck to save an Umbrella employee, and no offense, but I think you're totally batshit for wanting to . . . but I'll wait for you, okay? Go give the guy a Band-Aid or whatever and then meet me at the dock."

Surprised, Claire nodded. Less than she'd hoped for but more than she'd expected, particularly after his weird people-will-let-you-down rant—

—oh!

For the first time, it occurred to her why Steve might have said those things, why he was denying the trauma of what had happened, what was still happening. He was here by himself, after all . . . how could he not have abandonment issues?

Claire smiled warmly at him, remembering how angry she'd felt as a child when her father had died. Being snatched away from one's family couldn't be much better. "It'll be nice to go home," she said gently. "I bet your parents will be glad—"

Steve's sneering interruption was immediate and extreme. "Look, come to the dock or not, but I'm not going to wait all day, got it?"

Startled, Claire nodded mutely, but Steve was already striding out of the room. She wished she hadn't said anything, but it was too late . . . and at least now she knew what *not* to say. Poor kid, he probably missed his parents like crazy. She'd have to try to be a little more understanding.

With a last look around the strange little den, Claire started back toward the front door, wondering what to do about Rodrigo. Steve was right, Umbrella might already have a team on the way, they could tend to him, but she meant to get him stabilized before she left. She needed to find a vial of that hemostatic liquid; she didn't know much about triage herself, but he had seemed to think it would help.

She opened both of the other doors in the hallway on her way back to the lobby, stopping briefly at the first to gaze in at a number of portraits, some kind of pictorial history room for a family called Ashford. There was a shattered urn on the floor, but nothing else of interest. Behind the second door was an empty conference room, only a few scattered papers and silence.

Claire stepped back into the front hall, deciding that she should probably try the upstairs before retracing her steps; just above the bridge to the prison—and wasn't she looking forward to crossing *that* creaking nightmare again—there'd been a door she'd bypassed in order to keep up with Steve's trail . . .

A tiny red light on the floor caught her attention, like one of those laser pointer things, her geometry prof had used one. The small light jerked toward her and Claire looked up, followed a pencil-thin beam to—

Gah! She dove for cover as the first shot bit into the tiles mere inches from where she'd stood, ceramic shards flying. She crashed behind one of the ornamental pillars as the second shot thundered through the lobby, shattering more tile.

She scrambled to her feet, trying to make herself as tiny as possible, wondering if she'd actually seen what she'd thought she'd seen—a thin blond man with a rifle and laser sight, wearing what looked like a dress uniform jacket from a yacht club, deep red, complete with puffy white cravat and gold braid. Like a child's idea of what noble authority should wear.

"My name is Alfred Ashford," a pinched, snobby voice called out. "I am the commander of this base— and I demand that you tell me who you're working for!"

What? Claire wished she had something brilliant to

say, some snappy comeback, but she couldn't get any further than that.

"What?" she asked loudly.

"Oh, there's no point in your feigned ignorance," he continued, his jeering voice moving a little, as though he were descending the stairs. "Miss Claire Redfield. I know what you've been planning, I've known from the start—but you're not dealing with just anyone, Claire. Not when you're dealing with an Ashford."

He actually tittered, a high, girlish giggle, and Claire was suddenly absolutely positive that he was a whacko, she was talking to a whacko.

Yeah, and keep him talking, you don't want to lose his position. She could see the tiny red light flicker on the wall behind her, as he worked to keep the pillar in his sights.

"Okay, ah, Alfred. What is it that I'm planning?" She jacked the action on her semi as quietly as possible, making sure there was a round in the chamber.

It was as though she hadn't spoken. "Our legacy of profundity, supremacy, and innovation is beyond question," Alfred said haughtily. "We can trace our heritage to European royalty, my sister and I, and to some of the greatest minds in history. But then I don't suppose your masters told you that, did they?"

My masters? "I don't have any idea what you're talking about," Claire called out, watching the flickering red dot, deciding that she could dart a glance out from behind the pillar's other side, maybe get off a shot before he could target her. The longer Alfred talked, the more strongly she felt that meeting him face-to-face would be a bad idea. Dangerously mentally ill people were unpredictable at best.

He'd mentioned a sister . . . the children in that movie, with the dragonfly? She didn't have proof, but her instincts shouted a resounding *yes*. It seemed he'd stayed the course, from creepy kid to creep.

"Of course, if you were willing to surrender yourself to me now," Alfred purred, "I might be persuaded to spare you your life. Providing that you confess to treason against your superiors—"

Now!

Claire ducked her head around the pillar, gun up—

—and *bam,* wood and plaster exploded next to her face, the shot splintering the pillar's molding as she pulled back. She leaned heavily against the pillar, her breathing fast and gulping. If he'd been a hair more accurate . . .

"Aren't you the fast little rabbit," Alfred said, his amusement unmistakable. "Or should I say rat? That's what you are, Claire, a rat. Just a rat in a cage."

Again, that insane, unnatural giggle . . . but it was receding, following him back up the stairs. Footsteps, and then a door closed, and he was gone.

Well, doesn't that round out things nicely? What's a biohazardous disaster without a crazy or two? It'd almost be funny, if she wasn't so totally weirded out. Alfred was a fruit loop.

Claire waited a moment to be sure he was gone, then exhaled heavily, relieved but not relaxed. She wouldn't, *couldn't* relax until she was well away from Rockfort, leaving Umbrella and monsters and insanity far behind.

God, but she was tired of this shit. She was a second

year lit major, she liked dancing and motorcycles and a good latte on a rainy day. She wanted Chris, and she wanted to go home ... and since neither of those seemed likely at the moment, she decided she'd settle for a good, solid nervous breakdown, complete with screams and floor-pounding hysterics.

It was almost tempting, but that would have to wait, too. She sighed inwardly. Alfred had gone upstairs, so she thought she'd better check out that other door she'd passed back near the bridge, see if she could find something for Rodrigo there.

At least things probably won't get any worse, she thought dismally, feeling a strange sense of déjà vu as she opened the front door. It felt so much like Raccoon City ... but that had been a serious catastrophe, rather than an isolated disaster.

Big, fat difference. All of it bites.

Claire had no way of knowing that compared to what lay ahead, things hadn't even started to get bad.

FIVE

THE ALLEGED DOCK WASN'T REALLY A DOCK at all, much to Steve's disappointment, and there wasn't a boat in sight. He'd expected a long pier with pilings and seagulls, all that shit, and a half dozen ships to choose from, each of them stocked with full pantries and soft beds. Instead, he'd found a tiny, grungy platform that sat over an unpleasantly gray lagoon-ish area, protected from the ocean by a ridge of jagged rock that he could barely make out in the dark. There was a pulpit kind of thing with a ship's steering wheel stuck on it at the edge of the platform, probably some dumbass "monument to the sea" or whatever, a decrepit table with some trash on it, and a ratty, moldy old life jacket heaped in a corner, the once bright orange stained to a murky mustard color. Nothing bigger than a canoe was ever going to dock at this particular pier; in a word, lame.

Great. So how did all those people get off the island, backstroke? And if there's an air strip, where the hell is it?

Bad enough that now he had to find another escape, he'd also told Claire that he'd meet her here. He couldn't just take off, but he didn't want to stand around waiting, either.

You could still ditch her.

Steve scowled, irritably kicking at a rusted-out hunk of random machinery. Maybe she was a little nosy, a little naive . . . but she'd saved his ass, no question, and her wanting to go back to help some wounded Umbrella hand just because he'd set her free—that was . . . well, it was *nice,* it was a nice thing to do. Leaving her behind didn't seem right.

Not sure what to do next, he walked over to the mounted steering wheel (wasn't there some kind of sailor name for it, one of those port-starboard-ahoy words? He didn't know.) and gave it a spin, surprised at how smoothly it turned considering how crappy the rest of the "dock" was—

—and with a low mechanical hum, the platform beneath his feet abruptly detached from the rest and slid out over the water, as giant bubbles started to break the water's surface in front of him.

Christ! Steve held on to the wheel with one hand, pointed one of the gold Lugers at the rising bubbles with the other. If it was one of Umbrella's creatures, it was about to be breathing hot lead—

—and a small submarine rose up out of the water like a dark, metal fish, the hatch conveniently popping open directly in front of his feet. A runged ladder led down into the sub, which appeared to be empty. Unlike the worn-out surroundings, the little sub looked sturdy and well-maintained.

Steve stared at it, astounded. What was *this* shit? It was like some theme park ride, so weird that he wasn't sure what to think.

Is it any weirder than anything else I've dealt with today?

Point taken. The map he'd looked at back at the mansion had been vague, just a couple of arrows and the words *dock* and *airstrip* . . . and apparently you had to take a submarine ride to get there. Umbrella was one messed up company.

He stepped down onto the top rung and then hesitated, his skin still red from the last unknown he'd stepped into. He didn't want to drown any more than he'd wanted to get baked alive.

Ah, screw it, won't know 'til you try.

Again, point taken. Steve climbed down the ladder, and when he stepped off, he triggered a pressure plate in the floor of the sub. Above him, the hatch closed. He quickly stepped on it again, and the hatch reopened. It was good to know he wouldn't suffocate, at least.

The interior of the submarine was very plain, maybe as big as a large bathroom, bisected by the narrow ladder. There was a small padded bench on one side, the rear of the sub, and a simple control console in front.

"Let's see what we got here," Steve muttered, stepping up to the controls. They were ridiculously simple, a single lever with two settings—the handle was currently next to the upper setting, marked "main." The lower setting was marked "transport," and Steve grinned, amazed that it could be this easy. Talk about user-friendly.

He tapped the pressure plate again, sealing the hatch, wondering if Claire would be impressed by his discovery as he pulled the lever down. He heard a soft metallic *thunk* and then the submarine was moving, descending. There was a single porthole, but it was too dark to see anything besides a few rising bubbles.

The anticlimactic ride was over in about ten seconds. The sub seemed to stop moving, and he heard a sharper metallic sound coming from the hatch, like it was brushing against something—definitely not an underwater sound.

Onward and upward. The hatch opened as he started to climb the ladder, gun firmly in hand . . . and he stepped out onto a metal platform walled in glass or plexi, surrounded by black water on either side. There were a few steps leading down to a well-lit hallway, where only the left-hand wall was made out of water.

Yeesh. It was like the displays at some aquariums, where you could go through an underwater tunnel, look at the fish. He'd never liked those things, finding it way too easy to imagine the glass breaking just as a shark decided to cruise by . . . or something worse.

Enough of that. Steve stepped down into the hall and followed it around two bends, deliberately staring straight ahead. It was the first time since the attack on the island that he'd felt really nervous—not so much claustrophobia as a kind of primal fear, that something would come flashing out of the dark water toward the glass, an animal or something else—a pale hand, perhaps, or maybe a dead, white face pressing against the window, smiling at him—

He couldn't help it. He broke into a run, and when the corridor met a door that apparently led away from the water room, he called himself pussy but was vastly relieved, anyway.

He pushed the door open—and saw two, three ... four zombies in all, and all of them suddenly quite eager for his company. Each of them turned and began to limp or stagger toward him, the rags of their clothing—Umbrella uniforms, no question—hanging from their outstretched arms. There was a smell like dead fish.

"Unnnh," one of them moaned, and the others chimed in, the wails strangely gentle in a way, kind of sad and lost-sounding. Considering what Umbrella had put him through, he didn't feel a whole lot of sympathy. None, in fact.

The room was half-split by a wall, the three zombies on the left unable to see the lone ranger on the right ... though maybe they could, he thought, peering closer. Each of the trio had eyes that seemed to glow, a strange dark red. They reminded him of a movie he'd seen once, about a man with super X-ray vision, who saw all kinds of shit.

Guess we'll never know what they see. Steve took aim at the nearest, closed one eye, and *bam*, right through the ol' frontal lobe, a clean hole appearing in its gray-green forehead like magic. The creature's red eyes seemed to fade and go out as it dropped, first to its knees, then flat down on its face, *sploosh*. Gross.

The zombie's comrades took no notice, kept coming. The lone ranger's progress had been stopped by a desk; he continued to walk anyway, apparently not noticing that he wasn't going anywhere.

Steve took out the next in line same as the first, a one shot kill, but for some reason, he didn't feel all that great about it. Shooting them down like that. It hadn't bothered him before, back at the prison—then it had felt good, powerful even; he'd been stuck in that hellhole for long enough to be pretty righteously pissed, and having some control again had been like Christmas, like a great, big, Christmas present that some little kid had been waiting for all year, like he used to wait . . .

Shut up. Steve didn't want to think about it, it was bullshit. So he didn't feel like clapping every time he wasted another one of them, so what? All it meant was that he was getting bored.

He hurriedly shot the last two, the shots seeming louder than before, practically deafening. A quick look around for anything useful—if paper clips and dirty old coffee mugs were useful, he was sitting pretty—and he was ready to move on. There were two doors on the back wall, one on either side of the room; he picked left on general principles. He'd read somewhere that when given a choice, most people picked right.

After checking his ammo, he walked past a big, empty fish tank that dominated the left side of the room and cautiously pushed the door open, taking in as much as he could in a single glance. Dark, cavernous, smells of salt water and oil, nothing moving. He stepped inside, sweeping with the Luger—

—and laughed out loud, a rush of pure joy washing through his system as his laugh echoed back at him. It was a seaplane hangar, and there was one big-ass seaplane sitting right in front of him. Big to him, anyway, he'd mostly flown in a little twin-engine private plane.

Thoroughly pleased, Steve walked toward the plane, which sat just below the mesh platform under his feet. He was an inexperienced pilot, but figured he probably knew enough not to crash the thing.

First things first, board her and check fuel, general condition, learn the controls . . .

He stopped at the edge of the platform and looked down, frowning. He was at least ten feet above the front hatch, which looked to be locked down tight.

There was a bank of machinery to his left, a few panels lit up. Steve walked over and looked at them, smiling when he saw a control to power up the boarding lift. The system should also open the plane door, according to the tiny diagram.

"Presto," he said, flipping the switch. A loud and grating mechanical noise bellowed through the giant hangar, making him wince, but it stopped after a few seconds, as a two-man lift slid to a halt at the platform's edge.

He stepped onto the lift, studied the standing control panel—and started to curse, every bad word he could think of, twice. Next to a trio of hexagonally shaped spaces were the words, "insert proof keys here." No keys, no power.

They could be anywhere on the whole goddamn island! And what are the chances that all goddamn three of them will be goddamn together?

He took a deep breath, made himself calm down a little, and spent the next few minutes figuring out how the plane's controls were hooked up to the rest of the system, looking for a way to bypass the keys. And after a careful, thoughtful deliberation, he started cursing again. When he finally got tired of that, he resigned himself to the inevitable.

Steve turned around and started to search the area, peering into every dark crevice, formulating theories about where the proof keys might be as he ran his hands over the greasy, dust-slimed machinery cabinets—and he decided that he was definitely going to dance all over the bones of the next Umbrella employee he gunned down, just for working at such an unnecessarily complicated place. Keys and emblems and proofs and submarines; it was a wonder they ever got shit done.

The virus carrier was wearing a lab coat and its lower jaw had fallen off somewhere, or been broken off; it gurgled and spluttered horribly, its wormy tongue flopping limply across its neck. Claire couldn't tell if it had been a man or woman, although she supposed it didn't really matter. As pitiful as it was revolting, she put it out of its misery with a single shot to the temple and then searched the area—working laboratory office, small inventory room—before stepping back into the hall, discouraged at her overwhelming lack of success.

The entrance she'd walked back to from the mansion had opened up into a reasonably big courtyard, hard packed dirt and totally utilitarian—more like the prison than the palace, although even after searching a few rooms, she still couldn't figure out where she was, exactly; some kind of testing facility, maybe, or a training ground for guards or soldiers.

Maybe just a building designed to destroy hope, she thought blackly, looking toward the front door. She'd walked in maybe ten minutes ago, hoping that Rodrigo wasn't already dead, that Steve had found a boat, that Mr. Psycho Ashford and his sister weren't planning to blow up the island—and in just ten minutes, those hopes had been thoroughly stomped on. All she really wanted now was a goddamn bottle of medicine, because then she'd be one step closer to leaving.

She'd tried the upstairs first, undergoing an exciting little adventure that had shaved a few years off her life. All she'd found up there was a small, locked lab with a lot of broken glass on the floor, from what appeared to be ruptured holding tanks. She'd seen the damage through an observation window, and had been about to leave when some poor, bloody guy in an environmental suit threw himself at the glass. It had been his dying act; the suit obviously hadn't done him much good, his head had practically exploded, coating the inside of his helmet with gore. It hadn't done her heart much good, either, scaring her half to death, and the whole upstairs experience had been topped off by an emergency shutter lockdown, apparently triggered by the suit guy. She'd practically had to hurl herself down the stairs to avoid being trapped.

Whee.

Nine zombies she'd had to put down so far, three of them in lab coats or scrubs, and not even a cotton swab to show for it. Nothing in the locker room—and she'd looked through practically every damned one of the lockers, turning up jockstraps and porn, but little else— nothing in the odd little shower room, zip and zilch. She'd have thought that a pharmaceutical company might actually have a few pharmaceuticals lying around, but it was looking more doubtful by the moment.

Claire walked back to the long hall that branched off from the building's first floor, that opened into an outdoor courtyard. She'd hoped to find something for Rodrigo without having to leave the building proper, but there was no help for it.

If I get lost, I can just follow the trail of corpses back, she thought, walking quickly down the nondescript corridor. Not funny, but she wasn't feeling all that politically correct at the moment. She was starting to run low on ammo, too, which made her even less inclined to a positive frame of mind.

She stepped from the relative warmth of the hall into the mist-cloaked courtyard, smells of the ocean permeating the cold gray night. A small fire burned against one wall. The whole Rockfort facility was strangely laid out, she thought, an unlike mix of new and old. Inefficient, but interesting; the little courtyard was actually cobblestoned, definitely not a recent addition—

Claire froze. The narrow red beam of a laser scope sliced through the mist in front of her, swept toward her from somewhere above. A low balcony to her right, the stairs for it set against the east wall.

Stairs, cover!

It was all she had time to think before the little red dot

was stuttering across her chest. She threw herself out of the way as the first shot blasted through the cold air, burying itself in a miniature fountain of stone chips.

She rolled to her feet and sprinted for the stairs, the red light jerking back and forth, trying to find her. *Bam,* a second shot, it missed but was close enough that she could actually hear it cutting through the air, a high-pitched buzzing sound. She caught a glimpse of the shooter just before ducking behind the low stone balustrade, not surprised at all to see slicked-back blond hair and a red jacket trimmed in gold.

She was more angry than scared, that after all she'd been through, she hadn't been more careful—and that she'd almost been taken out by such a weird little elitist creep.

That stops right now. Claire raised her handgun over the stone railing and fired off two rounds in Alfred's general direction. She was immediately rewarded with a cry of shocked outrage. *Not so much fun when the peasants fire back, is it?*

Ready to capitalize on his surprise, Claire scrambled up three steps and risked a look over the rail—just in time to see him run through a door on the west wall, slamming it behind him.

She leaped up the stairs and took off after him, banging through the door and down a moonlit hall, shafts of cool light gently piercing the shadows. It wasn't a conscious decision to pursue him, she just did it, not wanting to stumble into any more of his ambushes. She could see what looked like a soda machine at the end of hall, could still hear his running footsteps—

—and heard a door slam just before she reached the corridor's end, a small room with two decrepit vending machines and two doors to choose between.

Claire hesitated, looking at either door—and then put her hands on her knees to catch her breath, giving up the chase. For all she knew, he was standing on the other side of one of those doors, just waiting for her to walk through.

Score one for the nutcase. Not a big victory, anyway. With any luck, she'd be off the island soon, Alfred Ashford just another bad memory.

After a moment she straightened, walking over to check out the vending machines—one for snacks, the other, beverages. She suddenly realized she was ravenous, and incredibly thirsty. When was the last time she ate?

The machines were both broken, but a couple of good, solid kicks circumvented the problem nicely; most of it was crap, but there were several bags of mixed nuts and a few cans of orange juice. Not exactly a steak dinner, but considering the circumstances, a bountiful harvest anyway. She ate quickly, stuffing a few unopened bags in her vest pockets for later, feeling more focused almost immediately.

So . . . door number one, or door number two? Eeny-meeny-miney-mo— The gray door, to the right of the corridor. She doubted that Alfred had the patience to still be waiting, but edged up to the door carefully just in case, pushing it open with the barrel of the 9mm.

Claire relaxed. A small, cozy room, couple of couches, an antique typewriter on a table, a large, dusty trunk in one corner. It seemed safe enough; Alfred must have gone through door number one. She stepped inside to search it, drawn toward a small heap of miscellaneous objects on one of the couches—and her breath caught in her throat, her eyes widening.

Thank you, Alfred!

Someone had dumped the contents of a fanny pack on the couch, the pack itself crumpled next to the pile, which included two sterile needles and a syringe, a pack of waterproof matches, half a box of 9mm rounds—and a small, half-filled bottle of the same hemostatic stuff Rodrigo had been out of, exactly what she'd been looking for. There were a few other odds and ends in the makeshift survival kit, a pen, a small flat screwdriver, a foil-wrapped condom . . . at the last, she rolled her eyes, grinning. Interesting, what some people considered absolute necessities. Her grin faded when she noticed the blood stains on the pack, but she still felt better than she had in days.

She reloaded the pack and strapped it low around her hips, transferring a few things over from her own woefully tight pockets. She could hardly believe her luck. The medicine was what she'd been most worried about, but it was also an incredible relief to find more ammo. Even a single clip's worth was a godsend.

A search of the rest of the room yielded up nothing more, not that she minded. She felt like the end was in sight, an end to this terrible and horrific night.

Get back to the prison, give the drugs to Rodrigo, then see if Steve's had any luck wrangling us a ride home, she thought happily, stepping out of the room. It had been a hard ride, but compared to Raccoon, this was a picnic—

The heavy rattle of the closing shutter whipped her

around, the moment of happiness blown as the corridor, her exit, was blocked off with a thundering *crash*.

No! Claire ran to the metal shutter, banged it once with her fist, already knowing that there was no chance. She was sealed in, the only possibility of escape now the one door she hadn't yet tried. The one Alfred had fled through.

"Welcome, Claire," a voice called out, as snotty and pretentious as she remembered, with the same snide undertone as before. There was an intercom box above one of the vending machines, in the upper corner of the room.

Howdy, Alfred, she thought dismally, unwilling to give him the satisfaction of her anger or fear. The whole compound was probably wired up for sound, she'd been stupid not to think of it, and just because she didn't see a camera, that didn't mean there wasn't one.

"You're about to enter a special playground, of sorts," Alfred continued, "and there's a friend of mine I'd like very much for you to meet; I think you'll play well together."

Fantastic, can't wait.

"Don't die too soon, Claire. I want to enjoy this."

He laughed, that insane, annoying, distinctly unnatural giggle of his, and then he was gone.

Claire stared blankly at the door she was supposed to go through, considering her options. It was probably the best thing Chris had ever taught her, that there were always options; they might all totally suck, but there was always a choice, regardless, and thinking over her alternatives now had a calming effect.

I can hide in the safe room, live on snack food and pop while I wait for Umbrella to show up. I can sit here and pray that some friendly party will miraculously come to my rescue. I can try to get through the steel shutter, or through one of the walls . . . with that screwdriver and some elbow grease, I can probably break out in about 10,000 years. I can kill myself. Or I can walk through Alfred's playground door, see what there is to see.

There were a number of variations, but she thought that basically summed things up . . . and only one of them made any sense.

Technically, none of them makes sense! Part of her howled. *I should be in my dorm room, eating cold pizza and cramming for some test!*

Objection noted, she thought dryly, reaching into her new pack for a full clip, tucking another in her bra for fast access. Time to see what Alfred and his underlings had been up to out here, see if Umbrella had finally come up with a formula for the perfect bio-organic warrior.

Claire stepped up to the door and paused, wondering if she should go into battle with some profound thought about her life, or love, wondering if she was ready to die . . . and decided that she could worry about all that stuff later. If there wasn't a later, she wouldn't have to worry about it, would she?

"Boy, am I smart," she murmured, and pushed the door open before she could lose her nerve.

Six

EVERYTHING WAS PERFECT.

The cameras were set so that he could watch from four different angles, all in full color, the "battle arena" well lit, his chair comfortable. He only regretted that he hadn't had time to return to their private residence, to watch the entertainment with Alexia by his side—although that had turned out to be advantageous, as well, a silver lining. The training facility's control room had cameras that could be re-angled with the touch of a button, ensuring the clearest possible view.

Alfred smiled, watching as Claire hesitated at the door, quite pleased with how his plan had come to fruition. She'd chased him as he'd hoped, stepped into his trap with hardly a struggle. He hadn't expected her to actually fire at him, but that was easily overlooked in retrospect. And truly, it made the anticipation for her upcoming death all the sweeter, the addition of a personal revenge aspect into the mix.

The OR1, a highly developed BOW specifically created for field combat, was one of Alfred's all-time favorites. The An3 Sandworm was impressive, to be sure, the standard Hunter 121s lethal and fast, but the OR1s were special—the human skeletal structure showed through, particularly in the face and torso, giving them the look of classic Death. Their skull faces leered out beneath corded ropes of real and synthetic tendon, like a neo grim reaper. They weren't just dangerous; the way they looked was terror inspiring, at the most basic level of instinct.

The island employees called them Bandersnatches, a nonsense word from some poem that was strangely fitting, considering their unique design and function. There were thirty of them at Rockfort, half of those in stasis, though Alfred had only been able to account for eight of them since the attack—

—*oh!* Claire was opening the door.

Elated, Alfred focused his full attention on the girl, his left hand on the camera controls, his right hovering over the lock functions for the storage areas.

Claire stepped onto the balcony of the large, open, two-story bay with gun in hand, trying to look everywhere at once. Alfred zoomed in on her face, wanting to fully appreciate her fear, but was disappointed by her lack of expression. After surmising that she was in no immediate danger, she seemed watchful, no more.

But when I push this button . . .

Alfred snickered, unable to contain his excitement, lightly stroking his right forefinger across the switches for the bay's two shuttered storage closets, one on the balcony, one bordering the freight elevator on the lower floor. At his whim, Claire Redfield would die. True, she wasn't important, her death as meaningless as her life had surely been—but it was the control that mattered, *his* control.

And the pain, the exquisite torture, the look in her eyes when she realizes that her existence is at its end . . .

Alfred controlled his body as tightly as he controlled his life, and prided himself on his ability to dominate his sexual desires, to feel nothing unless he chose to—but just thinking of Claire's death inspired in him a passion that was beyond physical lust, beyond words, even beyond the simple scope of man's awareness.

Alexia knows, Alfred thought, certain that his beautiful sister was watching, too, that she understood what could not be explained. In Claire's death, they would be as close as two people could ever be; it was the wonder of their relationship, the culmination of the Ashford legacy.

He couldn't contain himself another moment. As Claire took another cautious step into the center of the room, he first locked the door she'd come through, sealing off her escape—and then pressed the button for the second story shutter release.

Instantly, the narrow metal shutter not ten feet from where she stood slid open—and as Claire stumbled backward, trying to distance herself from the unknown threat, a fully matured Bandersnatch stepped out, ready to engage.

It was beautiful, the creature. Between seven and eight feet tall, its face was that of a grinning skeleton, its head set low and menacing. The disproportionately huge upper body supported its primary weapon—the right arm, as thick as one of its tree-trunk legs, longer than half its full body length at rest, the hand span big enough to cover an ordinary man's entire chest. Its left arm was withered, tiny and misshapen, but a Bandersnatch only needed the one.

Alfred had hoped for some exclamation from her, a curse or a scream, but she was silent as she retreated to what she believed to be a safe distance. She opened fire almost immediately.

The Bandersnatch roared, a rough guttural scream, and then performed its trick. Alfred had seen it a dozen times, but never tired of watching.

The massive right arm snapped toward Claire, probably fifteen feet away, the engineered muscles hyperextending, the elastic tendons and ligaments stretching—

—and it slapped Claire to the ground with scarcely any effort, the girl knocked sprawling before the Bandersnatch's arm snapped back into place.

Yes, oh, yes!

Claire crabbed backward as fast as she could, stopping only when her back hit the wall. Alfred zoomed in to see that a fine sheen of sweat had broken out across her face, but she still wore no expression beyond a kind of intense watchfulness. She pulled herself to her feet and sidestepped along the wall, moving fast, obviously not wanting to be knocked off the balcony by the creature's next blow.

Alfred grinned, ignoring the disappointment that her apparent lack of terror had brought about. She'd be out of wall in another few seconds, backed into a corner—

—and then a series of blows, beating her to death against the wall . . . or a simple neck snap, a grasp of her head and a single, solid shake . . . or will it toy with her, tossing her around like one of Alexia's ragdolls?

Alfred leaned in eagerly, changing the angle for one of the cameras, watching as the doomed girl raised her weapon, taking careful aim in spite of her hopeless position—

—bam!

The Bandersnatch shrieked even louder than the gunshot, shaking its head wildly, dark fluids rushing from its moving face. It sprayed the balcony walls with ichorous liquid, blood and other things, trying desperately to bring its arm up, to protect or comfort its wound. It all happened so fast, so violently, it was like watching a fountain geyser suddenly explode from a still lake.

The eyes. She went for its eyes.

Bam!

Claire shot again, and then again, and the Bandersnatch cried out in fury and new pain, still trying to grasp its own injured head as it stumbled around in a weaving circle . . . and then, to Alfred's shock, it collapsed to the floor, its writhings becoming less and less urgent, its scream becoming a hoarse, dying protest.

Stunned with disbelief, Alfred could finally see an emotion on Claire's face—pity. She moved to stand over the creature and shot once more, stilling it completely. Then she turned and walked toward the stairs, as casually as if she was walking away from a ladies' luncheon.

No-no-no-no!

This was wrong, all wrong, but it wasn't over, not yet.

Furious, he stabbed at the other switch, releasing the second creature from its enclosure, the shutter sliding open behind a stack of storage containers on the elevator level.

You won't be so fortunate this time, he thought desperately, still barely able to credit what he'd just seen. Claire had heard the second door open, but the stack of containers obscured her point of view, hiding the new menace. She was stopped at the foot of the stairs, holding herself very still, scanning for the exact source of the noise.

The second Bandersnatch stepped out of its closet and casually reached up, grasping a large metal crate at the top of a ten foot stack of them. It pulled itself up, seemingly without effort—and without Claire noticing, her attention too intently fixed on the shadowy corner opposite the stairs.

The Bandersnatch reached down for her. Claire saw it coming at the last instant, too late to get out of its way. The creature wrapped its muscular fingers around her head and lifted her up, studying her as a cat studied a mouse.

Or a rat, Alfred thought, some of his previous joy returning at the sight of the girl dropping her weapon and struggling to free herself, grasping at the OR1's steel grip with panicked hands—

—and Alfred's focus was broken at the sound of shattering glass somewhere off screen, and someone was shooting, the sudden flurry of noise and activity making the Bandersnatch shriek, making it drop Claire.

What's—?

The window, Alfred answered himself, watching in horror as the young prisoner, Burnside, threw himself into the camera shot, firing two handguns at once, blasting at the startled creature—startled, then screaming in agony as Claire scooped up her weapon and joined the fray. The Bandersnatch tried to attack, its arm whipping out toward the new assailant, but it was driven back by the sheer number of rounds being pumped into its body, finally slumping against a storage container. Dead.

Without consciously deciding to do it, Alfred reached for the freight elevator controls, a part of him remembering that there was at least one more OR1 below, as well as a number of virus carriers. The two youths stumbled as the floor beneath their feet began to go down, taking them to the basement of the training facility. There were no working cameras there, but enjoying their deaths was no longer Alfred's primary concern—not so long as they died.

Can't be, this can't be happening. The OR1s should have dispatched Claire and her meddlesome friend effortlessly, but they were alive and his pets had suffered and died. He tried to convince himself that the two would soon perish in the basement, which had been locked down and isolated since the first viral leak, but suddenly, nothing seemed certain anymore.

"Alexia," Alfred whispered, feeling the blood drain from his face, feeling his very being flush with shame. He had to make her see that it wasn't his fault, that his trap had worked perfectly, that the impossible had occurred . . . and he'd have to accept the subsequent coolness in her gaze, the undertone of disappointment in her sweet voice as she reassured him that she understood.

The only thing that surpassed his shame was a newfound hatred for Claire Redfield, burning brighter than a

thousand burning stars. No sacrifice was too great to se-
cure her torment, hers and that of her shining knight.

Until both had offered penitence in flesh and blood,
Alfred would not rest. He swore it.

"Steve, other side," Claire said, the instant the freight
elevator began to move. Steve nodded. Claire reloaded
and Steve clambered over two of the heavy crates, both
Lugers raised. As if by silent agreement, neither of them
spoke as the lift descended, both watching intently for
what came next.

He saved my life, Claire thought wonderingly, watching grease-smeared wall tracks slide past, blood still
screaming through her veins from when she'd realized
she would die. And Steve Burnside, who she'd written
off as a well-intentioned but troubled, barely competent
blowhard, had kept that from happening.

Though he may only have delayed the inevitable . . .

She didn't know what Alfred had in mind now, but
she wasn't looking forward to meeting any more of his
"friends." Two skull-faced, rubber band–armed freaks
had been more than enough. She'd been incredibly
lucky to get off with a couple of bruises and a sore neck.

Claire had expected the elevator to drop them into
some sort of BOW holding area, but she was pleasantly
disappointed. The massive lift simply came to a stop.
There was only one exit that she could see, and although
she harbored no illusions about how safe things would
be on the other side of that door, it seemed they were out
of danger for the moment.

"Hey, Claire, check it out!"

Steve climbed back over the boxes, holding what could only be some kind of a submachine gun, boxy, dark and deadly-looking with an extended magazine.

"It was behind one of the crates," Steve said happily. He'd already stuck the gold Lugers in his belt. "Nine millimeter, just like the Lugers and the guard weapons. Oh, by the way, here."

He reached into one of the outside pockets on his camo pants and pulled out three clips for the M93R. "I searched a couple of guards on my way back from the dock. I like the Lugers better, and now that I've got *this* . . . " He held up the new weapon, grinning, "I don't need the extra hardware. You can have the gun, too."

Claire gratefully accepted the clips and the weapon, not sure how to thank him for what he'd done, determined to try, anyway.

"Steve . . . if you hadn't shown up when you did . . ."

"Forget it," he said, shrugging. "We're even now."

"Well, thanks all the same," Claire said, smiling warmly.

He smiled back, and she saw a flicker of real interest in his gaze, a sincerity there that was quite different than his previous posturing. Not sure what to do about it, for him or for herself, she moved the conversation along.

"I thought you were going to wait at the dock," she said.

"It wasn't really a dock," Steve said, and told her what had happened since they'd separated. The seaplane was terrific news; having to deal with Umbrella's bizarre key fetish yet again wasn't so terrific.

". . . and when I couldn't find them, I thought I'd

wander over and see if you'd come across anything like that," he finished, shrugging again, working hard to look nonchalant. "That's when I heard the shots. How 'bout you, anything interesting? Besides meeting up with a couple of Umbrella's monsters, I mean."

"I'll say. Do you know anything about Alfred Ashford?"

"Only that him and his sister are total fruitcakes," Steve said promptly. "And that the guards are—*were* scared of him. I could tell, the way they avoided talking about him. He sent his own assistant to the infirmary, I heard. There was some whacked-out doctor working there, I guess, a lot of prisoners got taken to the infirmary and never came back. Doesn't take a genius, you know?"

Claire nodded, fascinated in spite of herself. "What about the sister?"

"I never heard much about her, except she's some kind of shut-in," Steve said. "No one even knows what she looks like. I think her name is Alexia . . . Alexandra, maybe, I don't remember. Why?"

She filled him in on her encounters with Alfred, followed by a brief synopsis of where she'd been and what she'd found. When she mentioned that she had the medication she'd been looking for, Steve scowled—and then blinked, his face clearly expressing a sudden change of heart.

"Maybe this Umbrella guy—"

"Rodrigo," Claire interjected.

"Okay, whatever," Steve said impatiently. "Maybe *he* knows something about these proof key things. Like where they are."

Good idea. "It would beat searching the entire island, wouldn't it?" Claire said. "You up for a trip back to the prison? Assuming we can get out of here, that is."

"Oh, I'll clear us a path," Steve said, not a trace of doubt in his voice. "You just leave that part to me."

Claire opened her mouth to comment on the pitfalls of overconfidence, particularly where Umbrella was concerned, then closed it again. Maybe it was his belief in himself that had carried him this far—that by not accepting the possibility of defeat, he was assuring himself a win.

Fine in theory, dangerous in practice. She'd be there to cover him, at least.

"We were on the first floor of the training facility," he continued. "Which means we're in the basement now . . . I know from my—"

Steve shook his head, flustered for some reason, but before she could ask about it, he continued on as if nothing had happened.

"There's a boiler room, and a sewer area . . . basically, we go that way," he said, gesturing at the door.

Claire decided not to point out that since it was the only door, she'd already come to that conclusion. "I'm right behind you."

"Stay close," Steve said roughly, walking to the door and looking back over the shoulder, trying to look fierce, his jaw set and his eyes narrowed. Claire was torn between irritation and laughter, finally choosing to think of it as endearing. Then he was opening the door, and the reality of their situation came back to her, floating in on the smell of gangrenous tissue. She stopped worrying

S.D. PERRY

about the little things, concentrating on the need to survive.

What Steve knew about guns he could sum up in about five seconds, but he knew what he liked. And he decided immediately upon pulling the trigger of his newest find that it was the shit, hands down.

He stepped out of the freight elevator ready to kick some rotten ass, and saw his opportunity less than ten feet away. There were five of them in all—well, five and a half, including the crawling mess on the floor over by the shelves—and all he had to do was *tap* the trigger, and then he was trying like hell to keep the weapon from flying out of his hand.

Bam bam bam bam bam bam bam—

He swept the kicking gun left to right, releasing the trigger as the last zombie's swiss-cheese brain parted company with its swiss-cheese head. It was all over in just a few seconds, so fast that it seemed unreal—like he'd coughed and a building had blown up or something.

Claire had taken care of the floor pizza during his sweep, and when he turned around, triumphant, he was a little surprised to see that she wasn't smiling . . . until he thought about it for a second, and then he felt a little ashamed of himself. As far as he was concerned, they weren't really *people* anymore. He knew that if he were ever infected he'd want someone to plug him, to keep him from hurting anyone else—not to mention granting him a fast death, rather than letting him rot on the hoof.

But they were human, once. What happened to them was entirely shitty and unfair, no question.

True, and maybe he should be more respectful—but on the other hand, the gun was extremely cool, and they were *zombies.* It was a touchy subject, not one that he was prepared to mess around with, but he decided he could at least not laugh about it in front of Claire. He didn't want her to think he was some bloodthirsty asshole.

He pointed at the door ahead and to the right, fairly sure that they were heading in the right direction, at least roughly. The way he figured it, they'd come out at least close to the front yard of the training facility.

Claire nodded, and Steve led the way once again, pushing the door open and stepping through. They were standing at the top of a half flight of open stairs, leading down into the boiler room. A room full of big, battered-looking, hissing machinery, anyway, Steve didn't actually know what a boiler looked like. There were four zombies milling around between them and the steps leading up and out, on the other side of the cold, hissing room.

Steve raised the machine gun and was about to fire when Claire tapped his arm, moving to stand beside him.

"Watch," she said, and pointed her 9mm at the zombie group—not quite, he saw, she was aiming low at something just past them—

—and pow, *BOOM,* three of the creatures went down, blackened and smoking. Behind them, what was left of a small, obviously combustible container, only jagged curls of splayed metal surrounded by a smudge of toxic smoke.

The fourth zombie had been hit, but not as hard. Claire took it out with a single head shot before speaking again.

"Saves ammo," she said simply, and brushed past him to walk down the steps. Steve followed, slightly awed by her but playing it detached, like he'd already thought of that. If there was one thing he knew about chicks, it was that they didn't like guys who mooned all over them, acting all goofy.

Not that I give a shit what she thinks about me, he told himself firmly. *She's just . . . kind of cool, is all.*

Claire reached the next door first, and waited until he caught up, nodded that he was ready. As soon as she opened it they both relaxed, he could see her shoulders loosen and felt his own heart beating again. A dark stone walkway, totally empty, open on one side. There was water running somewhere below, and some kind of a narrow gate straight ahead, like an old-fashioned elevator door.

"This is starting to seem a little too easy," Claire said softly.

"Yeah," Steve whispered back. So much for Alfie-boy's evil playground shtick.

They were about halfway across when they heard it, echoing up from somewhere in the black running waters below—a strangely high, piercing trill, inhuman but not like an animal, either. Whatever it was, it sounded extremely pissed—and from the splashing noises, it was coming closer.

Steve was ready to start shooting but Claire grabbed his arm and took off running, practically jerking him off his feet. They were at the lift in about two seconds, Claire ripping the gate aside and shoving him into a tiny elevator cab, jumping in after him and slamming the gate closed.

"Okay, jeez, you don't have to push," Steve said, rubbing his arm indignantly.

"Sorry," she said, pushing an errant strand of hair behind one ear, looking as rattled as he'd seen her get. "It's just—I've heard that sound before. Hunters, I think they're called, extremely bad news. There were a bunch of them loose in Raccoon."

She smiled shakily, which suddenly made him want to put his arm around her, or hold her hand or something. He didn't.

"Brings up some bad memories, you know?" she said.

Raccoon . . . that was the place that had been blown up a few months ago, if he remembered right, right before he'd come to Rockfort. The town's own police chief had done it. "Did Umbrella have something to do with Raccoon?"

Claire seemed surprised, but then smiled a little easier, turning her attention to the elevator controls.

"Long story. I'll tell you about it when we get out of here. So, first floor?"

"Yeah," Steve said, then changed his mind. "Actually, maybe we should go up to the second. That way we can look out over the yard, see what we'll be up against."

"You know, you're smarter than you look," Claire said teasingly, punching the button. Steve was still trying to think of a witty comeback when the elevator came to a stop, and Claire opened the door.

There was a shuttered lockdown door to their right, so they went left, the short hallway empty. There was only one door in that direction, too, but they were in luck, the knob turned when Claire tried it.

Again, there were no surprises. The door opened up to a cramped wooden balcony thick with dust, overlooking a big room full of junk—a rusted military Jeep, stacks of grungy old oil drums, broken boxes and the like. It seemed more like a storage shed than anything else, and though it was well lit, there were enough piles of crap that it was impossible to see if anyone was down there. There was, though, Steve could hear shuffling noises.

He took a few steps to the left, trying to see the corner beneath the balcony, and Claire followed. The boards creaked and shifted beneath their steps.

"Doesn't seem too sturdy—" Claire started, and was cut off by a giant, splintering *craaack,* pieces of the balcony floor flying up as both of them went down.

Shit—

Steve didn't even have time to tense for the impact, it was over so quick. He landed on his left side, jarring his shoulder, his left knee cracking against a random bit of wood.

Almost immediately, a pyramid of empty barrels fell over behind him, clattering hollowly to the ground— and Steve heard a zombie's hungry wail.

"Claire?" Steve called, crawling to his feet and turning, looking for her and the zombie. There she was amid the barrels, still down, rubbing one ankle. Her handgun was about ten feet away. Steve saw her eyes go wide and followed her gaze, a lone zombie teetering toward her—

—and all he could do was stare at it, his body suddenly a million miles away. Claire said something but he couldn't hear her, too intent on the virus carrier. It had been a big man, leaning toward fat, but someone had blasted off part of his gut. The open, sticky, belly wounds were seeping, the dark shirt made even darker by the almost uniform layer of blood that had soaked the cloth. It was gray-faced and hollow-eyed, like all of them, and had either bitten through its tongue or had been eating—his, its mouth was smeared with blood.

Claire said something else, but Steve was remembering something, a sudden, vivid flash of memory so real that it was almost like reliving the experience. He'd been four or five years old when his parents had taken him to his first parade, a Thanksgiving parade. He was sitting on his father's shoulder, watching the clowns go by, surrounded by loud, shouting people, and he'd started to cry. He couldn't remember why; what he remembered was his father looking up at him, his eyes concerned and full of love. When he'd asked what was wrong, his voice was so familiar and well-loved that Steve had wrapped his tiny arms around his father's neck and hidden his face, still crying but knowing he was safe, that no harm could come to him so long as his father held him—

"Steve!"

Claire, practically screaming his name—and he saw that the zombie was almost on top of her, its gray fingers closing around her vest, pulling her up to its drooling, bloody mouth.

Steve screamed, too, opening fire, the thunder of bullets ripping into his father's face and body, tearing him away from Claire. He kept firing, kept screaming until his father lay still and the thunder had stopped, only dry *clicks* coming from the gun, and then Claire was touching his shoulder, turning him away as he called out for his father, weeping.

They sat for a while. When he could speak, he told her about it, parts of it, his arms around his knees and head down. Told her about his father, who had worked for Umbrella as a truck driver, who had been caught trying to steal a formula from one of their labs. He told her about his mother, who had been gunned down by a trio of Umbrella soldiers in their own home, lay choking and bloody and dying on the living room floor when Steve came home from school. The men had taken them away, taken Steve and his father to Rockfort.

"I thought he was killed in the air strike," Steve said, wiping at his eyes. "I wanted to feel bad about it, I did, but I just kept thinking about Mom, about how she looked . . . but I didn't want him to die, I *didn't*, I . . . I loved him, too."

Saying it out loud made him start crying again. Claire's arm was around him but he barely felt it, so sad that he thought he might die. He knew he had to get up, he had to find the keys and go with Claire and fly the plane, but none of that seemed important anymore.

Claire had been mostly quiet, only listening and holding him, but she stood up now and told him to stay where he was, that she'd be back soon and then they could leave. That was okay, it was good, he wanted to be alone. And he was more exhausted than he'd ever been in his life, so tired and heavy that he didn't want to move.

Claire went away, and Steve decided that he should go looking for the proof keys soon, very soon, as soon as he stopped shaking.

SEVEN

IN THE COOL DARKNESS, RODRIGO HAD BEEN resting uneasily. Now he heard a noise out in the corridor, and forced himself to open his eyes, to get ready. He lifted his weapon, bracing his wrist on the desk when he realized he hadn't the strength to hold it up.

I'll kill anyone messes with me, he thought, more by habit than anything else, glad he had the gun even if he was already a dead man. A zombie guard had fallen down the stairs and crawled into the cell room sometime after the girl had left, but Rodrigo had killed it with a boot to the head and taken its weapon, still holstered on its broken hip.

He waited, wishing that he could go back to sleep, trying to stay alert. The gun eased his mind, took away a lot of his fear. He was going to die soon, it was inevitable . . . but he didn't want to become one of *them,* no matter what. Suicide was supposed to be a particularly awful sin, but he also knew that if he couldn't manage to wipe out an approaching virus carrier, he'd eat a bullet before he let it touch him. He was probably going to hell, anyway.

Footsteps, and someone was walking into the room, too fast. A zombie? His senses weren't working right, he couldn't tell if things were speeding up or he was slowing down, but he knew he had to shoot soon or he'd miss his chance.

Suddenly, a light, small but penetrating—and there she was, standing in front of him like some dream. The Redfield girl, alive, holding a lighter up in the air. She left it burning, set it on the desk like a tiny lantern.

"What're you doing here?" Rodrigo mumbled, but she was rummaging through a pack at her waist, not looking at him. He let the heavy gun drop from his fingers, closing his eyes for a second or a moment. When he opened them again, she was reaching for his arm, a syringe in one hand.

"It's hemostatic medicine," she said, her hands and voice soft, the prick of the needle small and quick. "Don't worry, you won't OD or anything, somebody wrote dosage numbers on the back of the bottle. It says it'll slow down any internal bleeding, so you should be okay until help comes. I'll leave the lighter here . . . my brother gave it to me. It's good luck."

As she spoke, Rodrigo concentrated on waking up, on overcoming the apathy that had taken him over. What she was telling him didn't make sense, because he'd let her go, she was gone. Why would she come back to help him?

Because I let her go. The realization touched him, flooded him with feelings of shame and gratitude.

"I . . . you're very kind," he whispered, wishing there was something he could do for her, something he could say that would repay her for her compassion. He searched his memories, rumors and facts about the island, *maybe she* can *escape . . .*

"The guillotine," he said, blinking up at her, trying not to slur his words too badly. "Infirmary's behind it, key's in my pocket . . . supposed to be secrets there. He knows things, puzzle pieces . . . you know where's the guillotine?"

Claire nodded. "Yes. Thank you, Rodrigo, that helps me a lot. You rest now, okay?"

She reached out and stroked his hair back from his forehead, a simple gesture but so sweet, so nice, he wanted to weep.

"Rest," she said again, and he closed his eyes, calmer, more at peace than he'd ever felt in his life. His last thought before he drifted off was that if she could forgive him after the things he'd done, show him such mercy as if he deserved it, maybe he wouldn't go to hell, after all.

Rodrigo had been right about secrets. Claire stood at the end of the hidden basement corridor, steeling herself to open the unmarked door in front of her.

The infirmary itself was small and unpleasant, not at all what she would have expected for an Umbrella clinic—no medical equipment to be seen, nothing modern at all. There was only a single examination table in the front room, the splintery wooden floor around it stained with blood, a tray of medieval-looking tools nearby. The adjoining room had been burned beyond recognition; she couldn't tell what purpose it had served, but it looked like a cross between a recovery room and a crematorium. Smelled like one, too.

There was a tiny, cluttered office just off the first room, a lone body sprawled in front of it, a man in a stained lab coat who had died with a look of horror on his narrow, ashen face. He didn't appear to have been infected, and since there were no virus carriers in the room and no obvious wounds, she guessed that he'd had a heart attack, or something like it. The contorted expression on his pinched features, bulging eyes and gaping, downturned mouth, suggested to her that he'd died of fright.

Claire carefully stepped over him, and found the first secret in the small office almost by accident. Her boot had nudged something when she walked in, a marble or stone that had rolled across the floor—which had turned out to be a most unusual key. It was a glass eye, one that belonged in the grotesque plastic face of the office's anatomical dummy, propped leering in the corner.

Considering what Steve had said, about no one coming back from the infirmary, and considering what she already knew about the kind of insanity that Umbrella seemed to attract, Claire wasn't surprised to find a hidden passage behind the office wall. A worn set of stone steps were revealed when she'd placed the eye back where it belonged, which hadn't really surprised her, either. It was a secret, a trick, and Umbrella was all about secrets and tricks.

So open the door, already. Get it over with.

Right. She didn't have all day. She didn't want to leave Steve alone for too long, either, she was worried about him. He'd had to kill his own father; she couldn't imagine the kind of psychological damage that would do to someone . . .

Claire shook her head, irritated with her own dawdling. It didn't matter that she was in a barren, frightening place where lots of people had apparently died, where she could feel the pervasive atmosphere of terror emanating from the cold walls, trying to wrap around her like a burial shroud . . .

"Doesn't matter," she said, and opened the door.

Immediately, three stumbling virus carriers started for her, drawing her attention, keeping her from really seeing the details of the large room they'd been trapped in. All three were badly disfigured, missing limbs and long, ragged strips of skin, their putrefying flesh flayed and raw. They moved slowly, painfully dragging themselves toward her, and she could see older scars on the exposed rotting tissue. Even as she targeted the first, the knot of dread in her stomach was expanding, making her feel sick.

It was over quickly, at least—but the terrible suspicion that had been growing in her mind, that she'd been hoping was false, was confirmed with a single good look around.

Oh, Jesus.

The room was strangely elegant, the muted lighting coming from a hanging chandelier. The floor was tiled, with a runner of finely woven carpet leading from the door to a kind of sitting area on the other side of the room. There was an overstuffed velvet chair and cherry wood end table there, the chair facing out so that someone sitting there would be able to see the entire room . . . which was worse than she could have imagined, worse than the mad Chief Irons's dungeon, hidden beneath the streets of Raccoon.

There were two custom-built water wells, one with a pillory built into its rail, a steel cage suspended over the other. Chains hung from the walls, some with well-used manacles attached, some with leather collars—some with hooks. There were a few elaborate devices that she didn't look at too closely, things with gears and metal spikes.

Swallowing back bile, Claire focused on the sitting area. The elegance of the furnishings and of the room itself made things worse somehow, adding a touch of warped ego to the obvious psychosis of its creator. Like it wasn't enough to enjoy torturing people, he—or she— wanted to observe it in luxury, like some mad aristocrat.

She saw a book on the end table and walked over to retrieve it, keeping her gaze fixed straight ahead. Virus zombies and monsters and useless death were all horrible things, tragic or frightening or both—but the kind of sickness represented by the chains and devices all around her was appalling to her very soul, because it made her want to give up her faith in humanity.

The book was actually a journal, leather bound with thick, high quality paper. The inner cover proclaimed that it was the property of a Dr. Enoch Stoker, no title or inscription otherwise.

"He knows things, puzzle pieces . . ."

Claire didn't want to touch the thing let alone read it, but Rodrigo had seemed to think it might help. She flipped through a few pages, saw that nothing was dated, and started scanning the narrow, spidery writing for a familiar word or name, something about puzzles, maybe . . . there, an entry that made several references to Alfred Ashford. She took a deep breath and started at the top.

We finally talked today about the details of my preferences and pleasures. Mr. Ashford wouldn't share his own, but he was most encouraging to me, as he's been since my arrival six weeks ago. He was informed at the beginning that my needs are unconventional, but now he knows everything, even the small things. I was uncomfortable at first, but Mr. Ashford—Alfred, he insists I call him Alfred—proved to be an eager audience. He said that he and his sister both strongly approve of research in the boundaries of experience. He told me that I should think of them as kindred spirits, and that here, I am free.

It was strange, describing aloud my feelings, sensations and thoughts that I've never shared. I told him about how it all started, when I was still a boy. About the animals I experimented with early on and later, the other children. I didn't know then that I was capable of killing, but I knew that the sight of blood excited me, that causing pain filled an empty, lonely space inside with profound feelings of power and control.

I think he understands about the screaming, about how important the screaming is to me and

Enough. This wasn't what she was looking for, and it was making her want to vomit. She turned a few pages, found another entry about Alfred and his sister, scanned over something about a private home—and went back, frowning.

Alfred attended one of my live autopsies today, and told me afterward that Alexia has asked after me, that she wants to know if I have everything I need. Alfred worships Alexia, will let no one near her. I haven't asked to meet her yet, and have no plans to do so; Alfred wants their private home to remain private, and to keep her all to himself. It's behind the common mansion, he told me, most people don't even know it exists. Alfred tells me things that no one else knows. I think he appreciates having an acquaintance with common interests.

He said that Rockfort has many places that require unusual keys—much like the eye he gave me—some new, some very old. Edward Ashford, Alfred's grandfather, was apparently obsessed with secrecy, an obsession shared by Umbrella's other founder, according to Alfred. He and Alexia are the only people alive who know all the hidden places at Rockfort, he said. Alfred had full sets of keys made for both of them when he took over his father's position. I joked that it's good to have a spare in case he ever locks himself out, and he laughed. He said that Alexia would always let him in.

I believe that twins often have a much deeper bond than other sets of siblings—that in a figurative sense, if you cut one, the other will bleed. I'd like very much to test this theory in a more literal way, regard-

ing pain levels. I've found that filling a fresh wound with cut glass and sewing it closed again is a

Sickened, Claire tossed the book aside and wiped her hands on her jeans, deciding that she had enough information to go on. She hoped quite sincerely that the corpse upstairs was Dr. Stoker's, that his black heart had failed him and it was the thought of going to hell that had frozen his face into a mask of terror—and she abruptly realized that she'd had more than enough of his atmosphere, that if she had to be in the infirmary for one more minute, she really was going to throw up. She turned and walked quickly to the door, was full on running by the time she reached the stairs. She took them two at a time, and sprinted through the upstairs room, not looking at the body, not thinking about anything but the need to get out.

When she hit the outside path that led back to the guillotine door, she collapsed against one wall and breathed in huge lungfuls of air, concentrating on keeping her gorge down. It took a couple of minutes before she was out of the danger zone.

When she felt ready, Claire plugged a fresh clip in her semi and started back toward the training facility. She realized that she'd lost the second weapon Steve gave her somewhere between the torture chamber and the front door, but there was nothing on Earth that would persuade her to step foot back inside. She was going to get Steve, and they would find those goddamn keys, and then they were getting the fuck away from the asylum that Umbrella had created at Rockfort.

* * *

Steve cried for a while, and rocked himself back and forth for a while, dully aware that he'd just done a very Big Thing—as far as lifetime experiences went, there was the small shit and then big and then capital B Big. There were some things that just changed people forever, and this was one of them. He'd had to kill his own father. Both his parents, good people who meant no harm, were dead. That meant there was no one in the world who loved him now, and it was that thought that kept repeating itself, making him cry and rock back and forth.

It was thinking about the Lugers that finally snapped him out of the private emotional hell he was in, that made him remember where he was and what was happening. He still felt entirely terrible, aching inside and out, but he started to tune back in to his environment, wishing that Claire was with him, wishing for a glass of water.

The Lugers. Steve rubbed at his swollen eyes and then pulled both of them from under his belt, staring down at them. It was stupid, unimportant—but somewhere in the back of his mind, he'd finally connected that when he'd taken the matched handguns off the wall, *that* was when he'd been locked in and the heat had gone on. It had been a trap . . . and as far as he could figure, the only purpose of a trap like that was to keep someone from taking the weapons.

Which means maybe they're useful for something besides shooting. Yeah, they were gilded and cool-looking and probably expensive, but the Ashfords obviously weren't hurting for money . . . and if the guns had some kind of sentimental value, why were they being used as part of a trap?

He decided that he wanted to go back and take a closer look at where they'd been hanging, see if putting them back did anything. It was a two-minute walk back to the mansion, tops, he could be there and back in five; Claire would wait for him if she got back first.

And if I stay here, I'll just keep crying. He wanted, *needed* something to do.

Steve stood up, feeling shaky and kind of hollow as he brushed dirt off his pants, unable to avoid looking over at where his father had died. He felt a rush of relief when he saw that Claire had covered him up with a piece of tarp. She was a great girl . . . though for some reason, he suddenly felt kind of weird about her, about telling her all that stuff. He wasn't sure how he felt.

He stepped outside, and was vaguely surprised to see that he wasn't in the front yard of the training facility. He was also vaguely surprised that in the small, high-walled square he *had* walked into was what appeared to be a WWII Sherman tank. Giant, mud-crusted treads, revolving turret with huge gun, the whole deal.

He might have been interested earlier, or at least more than just a little surprised—there was no reason at all for there to be a tank at the Rockfort facility—but now all he wanted to do was check out the Luger trap, see if he could at least contribute something toward getting them off the island. He felt kind of bad that Claire had been stuck with questioning the wounded Umbrella guy by herself, since it was his idea and all.

On the other side of the tank was a door that *did* open into the training yard. At least his sense of direction wasn't totally blown. It seemed darker than it had earlier; Steve looked up and saw that the sky had gone cloudy again, blocking the moon and stars. He was about halfway across the yard when he heard thunder, loud enough that the very ground seemed to quake a little beneath his feet. By the time he reached the other side, it had started to rain again.

Steve stepped up the pace, hanging a right at the exit and jogging for the mansion. The rain was heavy and cold, but he welcomed it, opening his mouth and turning his face to the sky, letting it wash over him. He was soaked in just a few seconds.

"Steve!"

Claire.

He felt his stomach knot up a little, turning to watch her approach. She caught up to him outside the door to the mansion's grounds, wearing a concerned expression.

"Are you all right?" she asked, studying him uncertainly, blinking rain out of her eyes.

Steve wanted to tell her that he was aces, that he'd shaken off the worst of it and was ready to get back to the zombie smackdown, but when he opened his mouth, none of that came out.

"I don't know. I think so," he said truthfully. He managed a half smile, not wanting her to worry too much but not wanting to talk about it, either.

She seemed to understand, swiftly changing the topic. "I found out that the Ashford twins have a private house hidden behind the mansion," she said. "And I'm not a hundred percent sure, but the keys we're looking for might be there. I think there's a good chance."

"You found all that out from the, uh, Rodrigo?"

Steve asked doubtfully. It was hard to imagine that an Umbrella employee would give that up to the enemy.

Claire hesitated, then nodded. "In a roundabout way," she said, and he suddenly had the impression that there was something *she* didn't want to talk about. He didn't push it, just waited.

"The problem is getting to the house," she continued. "I'm sure it's locked up tight. I was thinking we might poke around the mansion a little more, see if we can find a map or a passage . . ."

She pushed her dripping bangs out of her eyes, smiling. ". . . and, you know, get out of the rain before we get wet."

Steve agreed. They went through the entrance to the manicured grounds, stepping over a few corpses along the way. He filled her in on his idea about the Lugers, which she thought they should definitely pursue—although she also pointed out that with the Ashford family running the island, Umbrella's cute little puzzles didn't necessarily need to be logical.

They stopped at the front door to do what they could about their clothes, which turned out to be not much. Both of them were drenched, though they did their best to squeeze out the excess. Fortunately for both of them, their feet had stayed dry; wet clothes were a pain in the ass, but trying to get around in squelching boots seriously sucked the root.

Weapons up, Steve pushed the door open. Shivering, they stepped inside—

—and heard a door close, upstairs and to the right.

"Alfred," Steve said, keeping his voice low, "betcha money. What say we put a few holes in his sorry ass?"

He started for the stairs, the question rhetorical. That loony craphound needed to be dead, for more reasons than Steve could count.

Claire caught up to him, put a hand on his shoulder. "Listen, some of the stuff I found back at the prison . . . he's not just crazy, he's seriously deranged. Like serial killer deranged."

"Yeah, I got that," Steve said. "All the more reason to take him out ASAP."

"Just . . . let's just be careful, okay?"

Claire seemed worried, and Steve felt protective all of a sudden, big time.

Oh, yeah, he's going down, he thought grimly, but nodded for Claire's sake. "You got it."

They moved quickly up the stairs, stopping outside the door they'd heard close. Steve stepped ahead of Claire, who cocked an eyebrow but said nothing.

"On three," he whispered, turning the knob very slowly, relieved that it was unlocked. "One—two—*three!*"

He shouldered the door, hard, bursting into the room and sweeping with the machine pistol, ready to shoot the first thing that moved—but nothing did. The room, a softly lit office lined with bookshelves, was empty.

Claire had gone in and turned left, past a couch and coffee table on the north wall. Disappointed, Steve stepped after her, expecting another door to another hall, so sick of the stupid mazes all over the place that he could just shit—

He stopped and stared, exactly what Claire was doing. Perhaps ten feet away was a wall, a dead end—

with two empty spaces set in a plaque at about chest level, indentations shaped like Lugers.

Steve felt a flush of adrenaline, of victory. He had no rational reason to believe that they'd just found the way to the Ashford's private residence, but he believed they had, anyway. So, it seemed, had Claire.

"I think we've got it," she said softly, "betcha money."

EIGHT

OH, WOW. THIS IS . . . WOW, CLAIRE THOUGHT.

"Wow," Steve whispered, and she nodded, feeling entirely out of her depth as she took in their new environment. Had she said serial killer crazy? *More like a serial killer convention.*

There'd been another puzzle after the Lugers had opened the wall, having to do with numbers and a blocked passage, but they'd ignored it completely—with both of them pushing, the passage wasn't blocked for long. Outside once again, they could see the private house, perched on a low hill like some brooding vulture in the pouring rain. It was a mansion, really, but nothing like the one they'd just left—it was much, much older, darker, surrounded by the decrepit ruins of what had once been some kind of a sculpture garden. Stone cherubs with blind eyes and broken fingers watched them wend their way toward the house, gargoyles with eroding wings, shattered pieces of marble underfoot.

Creepy, definitely . . . but this is so far beyond creepy, it's not even in the same category.

They stood in the foyer, unlit but for a few strategically placed candles. There was a smell of must in the air, an old smell like dust and crumbling parchment. The floor was plushly carpeted, what they could see of it, but so ancient that it had been worn threadbare in many places; it was hard to make out any color beyond "dark." What had once been a grand staircase was directly in front of them, sweeping up to second and third floor balconies; there was still a kind of shabby elegance to its time-blackened banisters and sagging steps, as there was in the dusty library to their right, in the faded, ornately framed oil paintings hanging from flocked walls. The word *haunted* would have described it perfectly . . . except for the dolls.

Tiny faces stared out at them from every corner. China dolls of fragile porcelain, many of them chipped or discolored, dressed for high tea in water-stained taffeta. Plastic children with roll-open plastic eyes and pursed pink mouths. Rag dolls with strange button faces, bits of stuffing poking out of withered limbs. There were jumbled piles of them, stacks of them, even a few featureless cloth babies impaled on sticks. There was no sane order to their placement that Claire could see.

Steve nudged her, pointing up. For just a second, Claire thought she was looking at Alexia, hanging from the eaves—but of course it was another doll, life-size, this one dressed for her bizarre lynching in a simple party dress, flowered hem floating around her slender synthetic ankles.

"Maybe we should—" Claire started—and froze, listening. The sound of someone talking filtered down to them from upstairs, a woman's voice. She sounded irate, the cadence of her speech rapid and harsh.

Alexia.

The angry voice was followed by a kind of pleading, whining tone which Claire immediately recognized as Alfred's.

"Let's drop in for a chat," Steve whispered, and without waiting for a response, he headed for the stairs. Claire hurried after him, not at all sure it was a good idea, but not wanting to let him go it alone, either.

The dolls watched them ascend in silence, staring after them with lifeless eyes, keeping their vigil and their peace as they had for many years.

Alfred never felt closer to Alexia than when they were together in their private rooms, where they'd laughed and played as children. He felt close to her now, too, but was also deeply distraught by her anger, wanting desperately to make her happy again. It was his fault, after all, that she was upset.

". . . and I simply don't understand why this Claire person and her friend are proving to be such a trial for you," Alexia said, and in spite of his shame, he couldn't stop watching her with adoring eyes, as she gracefully swept across the room in her silken gown. His twin was breathtakingly refined in her displeasure.

"I won't fail you again, Alexia, I promise—"

"That's right, you won't," she said sharply. "Because I intend to take care of this matter myself."

Alfred was aghast. "No! You mustn't risk yourself, darling, I . . . I won't allow it!"

Alexia glared at him for a moment—then sighed, shaking her head. She stepped toward him, her gaze soft and loving once more.

"You worry too much, brother," she said. "You must remember yourself, remember to always embrace difficulty with pride and vigor. We are Ashfords, after all. We—"

Alexia's eyes widened, her face paling. She turned toward the window overlooking the corridor outside, slender fingers rising anxiously to the choker at her throat. "There's someone in the hall."

No!

Alexia had to be kept safe, *no one must touch her, no one!* It was Claire Redfield, of course, finally here to fulfill her assignment, to assassinate his beloved. Frantic to protect her, Alfred spun around, searching—there, the rifle was leaning against Alexia's dressing table, where he'd left it before opening the attic room passage. He strode toward it, feeling her fear as his own, their anxiety shared as if they were one.

Alfred reached for the weapon—and hesitated, confused. Alexia had insisted on handling the situation, she might be angry again if he interfered . . . but if something happened to her, if he lost her . . .

—The handle to the door rattled suddenly, just as Alexia stepped forward, snatching up the rifle herself. She barely had time to lift it before the door burst open with a crash. It was the first time in almost fifteen years that their inner sanctum had been breached, and Alexia was so shocked by the intrusion that she didn't fire right away, not wanting Alfred to be hurt, not wanting to die. The two prisoners had guns, had them pointed directly at her.

Alexia collected herself, refusing to be terrorized by two children—who were both staring at her strangely, their peasant faces expressing confusion and surprise. Apparently they weren't used to audiences with their betters.

Use it to your advantage. Keep them off their guard.

"Ms. Redfield, and Mr. Burnside," Alexia said, her chin held high, her tone as dignified as the Ashford name required, "we meet at last. My brother tells me that you've caused quite a lot of trouble."

Claire stepped toward her, the barrel of her gun lowering slightly as she searched Alexia's face. Alexia stepped back involuntarily, repelled by her dripping clothes and forward manner, but kept her eye on Claire's weapon. The girl was too intent on her study, as was the young man, who had crowded in behind Claire.

Alexia moved back another step. She was cornered, trapped between her dressing table and the foot of her bed, but again, it was to her advantage. *When they've been lulled into thinking I'm not a danger . . .*

"*You're* Alexia Ashford?" The boy asked, amazed or awed, his mouth open.

"I am." She wouldn't be able to tolerate such rudeness for much longer, not from one so far beneath her.

Claire nodded slowly, still looking into her eyes boldly, impertinently. "Alexia . . . where's your brother?"

Alexia turned to look at Alfred—and started, because he was nowhere in the room. He'd left her to confront these people by herself.

No, it can't be, he'd never desert me like this—

Movement to her right—but she realized as she turned to look that it was only the mirror, and . . . and . . .

Alfred was looking back at her. It was her face, lips painted and lashes curled, but his hair, his jacket. She raised her right hand to her mouth, shocked, and Alfred did the same, watching her. Feeling her astonishment.

As if they were one.

Alexia screamed, dropping the rifle, forgetting all about the two trespassers as she pushed past them, not caring if they shot her or not. She ran for the door that connected her room to Alfred's, screaming again as she spotted the long, blond wig on the floor, the beautiful gown crumpled next to it.

Weeping, she pushed through the door, a revolving panel, fleeing across Alfred's room—

—my room—

—not sure where she was going as she stumbled through the corridor, running for the stairs. It was over, it was all over, everything ruined, everything a lie. Alexia had gone away and never come back, and he had—she was—

The twins suddenly knew what had to be done, the answer shining through the spinning blackness of their mind, showing them the way. They reached the stairs and headed down with plans forming, understanding that it was time, that they truly would be together now because it was finally time.

But first, they'd destroy it all.

"Holy shit," Steve said, and when he couldn't think of anything else to say, he repeated it.

"So Alexia was never here," Claire said, wearing the same dumbfounded expression that he suspected was on his own face. She walked over and picked up the wig, shaking her head. "Do you think she ever existed at all?"

"Maybe as a kid," Steve said. "There was this older guard at the prison who said he'd seen her once, like twenty years ago. Back when Alexander Ashford ran things."

For a few seconds, they just stared around the room, Steve thinking about how Alfred had looked when he'd seen himself in the mirror. It had been so pathetic, he'd almost felt bad for the guy.

Thinking all this time that his sister lived here—probably the only person in the world who didn't think he was a total prick—and it turns out he doesn't even have that . . .

Claire shook herself like she'd had a sudden chill and got them back on track. "We'd better look for those keys before one of the twins comes back."

She nodded toward the narrow ladder at the head of the bed. It led up to an open square in the ceiling. "I'm going to look up there, you check around here."

Steve nodded, and as Claire disappeared through the opening in the ceiling, he started to open drawers and rifle through them.

"You wouldn't believe what's up here," Claire called

down, just as Steve discovered a drawer full of silky lingerie, panties and bras and a bunch of other stuff he couldn't begin to guess at.

"Ditto," he called back, wondering what lengths Alfred had gone to in order to play Alexia. He decided he didn't really want to know.

He heard Claire thumping around overhead as he went to the dressing table and started to dig. A lot of makeup and perfume and jewelry, but no proofs or emblems, not even a house key.

"Nothing yet, but . . . hey, there's another ladder!" Claire shouted.

Good thing, Steve thought, finding a box of stationery with little white flowers on the paper. He was getting more nervous about Alfred coming back, and wanted to get out of his freaky room of sister psychosis as soon as possible.

There was a tiny white card on top of the stationery envelopes. Steve picked it up, noting the strong, feminine hand.

Dearest Alfred—you are the brave, brilliant soldier, ever fighting to reinstate the Ashford name to its former glory. My thoughts are with you always, beloved. Alexia.

Ick. Steve dropped the card, making a face. Was it just him, or had Alfred created a seriously unnatural relationship with his imagined sister?

Yeah, but it wasn't real, it wasn't like they could do anything . . . physical. Double ick. Again, Steve decided he'd rather not know—

"Steve! Steve, I think I found them! I'm coming down!"

Overwhelmed by an instant rush of hope and optimism, Steve grinned, turning toward the ladder, the words music to his ears. "No shit?"

Claire's shapely legs appeared, her voice much clearer, and he could hear the same excitement in her response as she quickly descended. "No shit. There was this little merry-go-round up there, and an attic room above that—oh, and you gotta check out this dragonfly key—"

An alarm suddenly started blaring, echoing through the giant house, loud and insistent. Claire jumped off the bed, holding three proof keys and a slender metal object in her hand. They locked gazes, exchanging a look of confused fear, and Steve realized he could hear the alarm outside, too, with the hollow, metallic sound of an announcement being made over a cheap sound system. It sounded like it was being broadcast over the entire island.

Before either of them could say a word, a calm voice began speaking through the bleating sirens, cool and female, the voice of a recorded loop.

"The self-destruct system has been activated. All personnel evacuate immediately. The self-destruct system has been activated. All personnel . . ."

"That bastard," Claire spat, and Steve was right there with her, silently cursing the pompous little freak—but only for about two seconds. They had to get to that plane.

"Go," Steve said, scooping up Alfred's rifle and putting his hand on Claire's back, urging her toward the door. Umbrella's Rockfort Training Facility and Detainment Center—the place where Steve had grieved his mother and lost his father, where the last descendant of the Ashford line had quietly gone mad and Umbrella's enemies had unleashed the beginning of the end—was about to go bye-bye, and he didn't particularly want to be around when it did.

Claire didn't need any advice on the matter. Together, they hustled through the door and ran, leaving the sad remnants of Alfred's twisted fantasy behind.

After triggering the destruct sequence at the common mansion, Alfred and Alexia hurried to the main control room, Alexia taking over to work the complicated console. All around them, lights flashed and the computer droned instructions over the sirens. It was all quite the ado, annoying to her but surely terrifying to the assassins.

Alexia had an escape plan, a key to the underground room where the VTOL jets were kept, but she had to know that the peasant children would be left behind. Until she was certain that they would die, she and Alfred couldn't leave.

Oh, they'll die, she thought, smiling, hoping that they weren't caught in any of the direct explosions. Better that they should be wounded by flying debris, that they should lie in torment as their lives slowly ebbed away . . . or perhaps the island's surviving predators would stalk and kill them, swallowing them down in great bloody chunks.

Alexia pulled up the security system cameras for the common mansion and grounds, eager to see Claire and her little knight cowering in fear, or screaming in panic. She saw neither; the mansion was empty, the lights and sounds of the imminent disaster carrying on uselessly, alerting bare corridors and closed rooms.

They might still be in our home, too afraid to leave, desperately hoping that the destruction will bypass them there . . . It wouldn't, of course, there was nowhere on the island that wouldn't be affected—

Alexia saw them then and felt her good humor disappear, her hatred boiling back into rage. The screen showed them at the submarine dock, the boy spinning the wheel. The sky was starting to lighten, shading from black to deep blue, the setting moon's pale light defining their sly and furtive scheming.

No. There was no chance for them. True, the empty cargo plane was still docked, the bridge raised, but Alfred had thrown the proofs into the sea after the air strike. They couldn't possibly believe that they had a chance . . .

. . . except they were in my private rooms.

"No!" Alexia shrieked, pounding her fist on the console, furious. She would not have it, would *not!* She'd kill them herself, claw their eyes out, tear them up!

There's the Tyrant, Alfred whispered in her ear.

Alexia's rage turned to passion, to exhilaration. Yes! Yes, there was the Tyrant, still in stasis! And it was intelligent enough to follow directions, provided they were simple, provided one pointed it the right way.

"You won't escape!" Alexia shouted, laughing, twirling around in joy and victory . . . and after a moment, Alfred joined in, unable to deny how deeply, wonderfully satisfying it was going to be, as the computer changed its tune and began the final countdown.

Their run to the plane was a blur—a mad dash out of the Ashfords' terrible home and down the rain-slick hill, to the mansion and down stairs, down more stairs to a tiny dock where Steve called up the submarine. Every step of the way, the alarms drove them faster, the continuous vocal loop reminding them of the obvious.

Just as they were climbing out of the sub, the bland female voice stopped repeating itself and began a new message—and though the words weren't exactly the same, Claire had a sudden vivid memory of Raccoon, of standing on a subway platform as another self-destruct loop had announced that the end was near.

"The self-destruct sequence is now active. There are five minutes until initial detonation."

"Well, that blows," Steve said, the first thing he'd said since they'd left the private mansion. And in spite of her fear that they wouldn't make it in time, in spite of her exhaustion and the horrible memories she knew she'd be taking away with her, Steve's deadpan utterance struck her as hilarious.

It does blow, doesn't it?

Claire started laughing, and though she tried to put an immediate stop to it, she couldn't quite manage. It seemed that even imminent death couldn't stop the giggles. That, or hysteria had turned out to be a lot funnier than she would have expected . . . and the look on Steve's face wasn't helping.

Hysterical or not, she knew they had to move. "Go," she choked, motioning him forward.

Still looking at her as though she'd lost her mind, Steve grabbed her arm and pulled her along with him. After a few stumbling steps—and the realization that her laughing fit might kill them both—Claire got hold of herself.

"I'm okay," she said, breathing deep, and Steve let her go, a look of relief crossing his pale face.

They ran down some stairs and through a kind of underwater tunnel, and as they reached the door at its end, the computer informed them that another minute had passed, that they had only four left. If there'd been any chance that she might start laughing again, that killed it.

Steve pushed the door open and jogged left, both of them leap-frogging over a trio of dead bodies, all virus carriers, all in Umbrella uniforms. Claire thought of Rodrigo suddenly, and her heart twisted. She hoped that he'd be safe where he was, or that he was well enough to get away from the compound . . . but she couldn't kid herself about his chances. She silently wished him luck and then let it go, following Steve through another door.

Their journey had ended in a huge, dark, metal-lined cavern, a hanger for seaplanes, and their hope of escape was sitting right in front of them—a smallish cargo plane floating just beneath the grid platform they were on. Not far to the right, blue predawn light defined the giant gateway that opened into the sea.

"Over here," Steve said, and hurried toward a small lift at the edge of the platform, one with a standing control board. Claire joined him, fumbling the three emblem proofs out of her pack.

"The self-destruct sequence is now active. There are three minutes until initial detonation."

The control board had a panel on top with three inset hexagonal spaces. Steve grabbed two of the proofs and together, they pressed all three of them home.

Oh, man, please please please—

There was an audible *click*—and the panel's switches lit up, a deep hum coming from the body of the standing machinery. Steve laughed, and Claire realized she'd been holding her breath when she was suddenly able to breathe again.

"Hang on," Steve said, and swiped his hand over the panel, flipping them all over.

With a small jerk, the lift began to lower at an angle, as the plane's rounded side door opened, folding down to create a stepladder. Claire felt like it was all happening in slow motion, a kind of unreality to it as the lift met the base of the steps, jerking again to a stop; it was hard to believe that it was finally happening, that they were actually going to make it off Umbrella's cursed island.

To hell with believing it, just go!

They boarded the plane, Steve running forward to get it flight ready while Claire quickly checked out the rest of it—a large, mostly empty cargo area constituted the bulk of the plane, sealed off from the cockpit by a soundproof metal hatch. There weren't any creature comforts beyond a closet with a port-o-john behind the pilot's seat, but there was a footlocker at the rear of the cockpit that contained two plastic gallon jugs of water, much to Claire's relief.

Though muffled, they could still hear the recording resonating through the hanger as Steve found the controls for the door, the hatch lifting and sealing as the countdown went to two minutes. Claire hurried to his side, her heart really starting to pound; two minutes was nothing.

She wanted to help, to ask what she could do, but Steve's full concentration was on the instrument panel. She remembered what he'd said about "iffy" flying skills, but since she didn't have any at all, she wasn't complaining. The seconds ticked past and she had to force herself not to start babbling nervously, not to do anything that might distract him.

The plane's engines had been rumbling, the sound getting steadily louder and higher-pitched, Claire's nerves tightening to match—and when the dreaded computer female spoke up again, Claire found herself gripping the back of Steve's chair, her knuckles white.

"There is now one minute until initial detonation. 59 . . . 58 . . . 57 . . ."

What if it's too complicated, what if he can't do it? Claire thought, fairly certain she was about to explode.

"44 . . . 43 . . ."

Steve straightened abruptly, grabbing a gear shift–looking thing to his right and nudging it forward before placing his hands on the yoke. The engine sounds got much louder, and slowly, very slowly, the plane started to move.

"You ready yet?" he asked, a grin in his voice, and Claire nearly collapsed with relief, her knees weak with it.

"30 . . . 29 . . . 28 . . ."

The plane edged forward beneath a low metal bridge, close enough to the door now that she could see small waves breaking against the metal siding. There was a loud *thump* overhead, as though the bridge had scraped the top of the plane, but they kept moving, slow and steady.

"17 . . . 16 . . ."

As Steve steered into the open water, the countdown reached ten . . . and then was too far away to be heard, as the engines got impossibly louder and they picked up speed, the smooth ride turning bumpy as they started to run over the waves. There was just enough light in the sky now for Claire to see the island's shore off to their right, rocky and treacherous. There were low cliffs bordering much of Rockfort, rising up out of the water like rough fortress walls.

Right before Steve started to pull back on the yoke, to lift the speeding plane up and away, Claire saw the first explosions, the sounds hitting a second later—a series of deep, thundering *booms* that quickly grew distant, dropping off as Steve gently raised them up.

As the cargo plane took to the air, giant billows of black smoke rose into the early dawn, casting shadows over the disintegrating compound. Flames were catching everywhere, and though she didn't know the exact layout of what she was looking at, she thought she saw the Ashfords' private home being gutted by fire, an immense orange light rising up behind what was left of the mansion. There were still structures standing, but immense pieces of them were suddenly missing, blown into rubble and dust.

Claire took a deep breath and let it out slowly, feeling knotted muscles begin to unclench. It was all over. Another Umbrella facility lost, because of the scientific integrity they continued to violate, because of a moral vacuum that seemed to be an elemental component of the company's policies. She hoped the tortured, twisted soul of Alfred Ashford had finally found some kind of peace . . . or whatever it was he truly deserved.

"So, where to?" Steve asked casually, and drawn back from her wandering thoughts, Claire turned away from the side window, grinning, ready to kiss the pilot.

Steve caught her gaze with his, also grinning—and as they looked into each other's eyes, the seconds stretching, it occurred to her for the first time that he wasn't just a kid. No kid would look at her the way he was looking at her now . . . and in spite of her firm decision not to encourage him, she didn't look away. He was a good-looking guy, definitely, but she'd spent most of the last twelve hours thinking of him as an obnoxious kid brother—not exactly easy to get past, even if she wanted to. On the other hand, after what they'd been through together, she also felt very close to him in a way that was solid, strong, an affection that seemed perfectly natural and . . .

Claire broke the eye contact first, looking away. They'd been free and safe for all of a minute and a half; she wanted to digest that for a little while before moving on.

Steve returned his attention to the controls, looking a little flushed—and there was another *thump* on the roof, like back in the hanger.

"What *is* that?" Claire asked, looking up as though she actually expected to see something through the metal.

"No idea," Steve said, frowning. "There's nothing up there, so—"

CRUUNCH!

The plane seemed to bob in the air and Steve hurried to compensate, as Claire instinctively looked behind them. The destructive sound had come from the hold.

"The main cargo hatch came open," Steve said, tapping at a small flashing light on the console, punching another button. "I can't get it to close."

"I'll check it out," Claire said, and at Steve's unhappy

expression, she smiled. "You just keep us in the air, okay? I promise not to jump."

She turned toward the hold, and as soon as Steve looked away, she casually grabbed the rifle hanging off the back of the copilot's chair, the one Alfred had dropped. She still had the semi, but the laser sight on the rifle meant pinpoint accuracy—and since she didn't want to shoot the plane full of holes, the .22 was a better choice. There had been a monster or two on the island, and maybe they'd ended up with a stowaway, but she didn't want Steve to worry, or get involved. They both needed him at the controls.

Whatever it is, I'll have to take care of it, she thought grimly, reaching for the door handle. Really, she was probably overreacting to some minor malfunction, a loose roof panel and a broken hinge. She opened the door—

—and leaped inside, slamming it behind her before Steve could hear the noise, *so much for minor—*

The entire rear of the hold was gone, the hatch torn away, clouds and sky whipping past at incredible speed. Confused, Claire took a single step forward—and saw what the problem was.

Mr. X, she thought wildly, remembering the monstrous thing in Raccoon, the relentless pursuer in the long, dark coat—but the hulking creature straddling the hydraulic track wasn't the same. It was humanoid, giant-sized and hairless like the X monster, its flesh similar, an almost metallic dark gray—but it was also taller and more muscular, built like an eight-foot-tall bodybuilder, its shoulders impossibly broad, its abdomen rippled with muscle. It was sexless, a rounded hump at its groin, and the hands weren't human hands, were far more lethal. Its left fist was a metal-spiked mace bigger than her entire head, its right hand a hybrid of flesh and curving knives, two of them at least a foot long.

And it's not wearing a coat, she thought randomly, as the monster turned its cataract-white eyes to look at her before throwing its head back and roaring, an explosive howl of blood lust and fury.

Terrified but determined, Claire raised her suddenly pathetic weapon as the creature started for her, and put the red dot on its right unicolor eye. She squeezed the trigger—

—and heard the dry *click* of an empty chamber, deafeningly loud even over the raging winds that spun past the damaged plane.

Nine

THERE WASN'T A CURSE WORD STRONG enough
to accurately express her dismay. Claire instantly
dropped the useless weapon and ran, dodging to the
right, not wanting to end up trapped in the corner, unable
to believe that she hadn't thought to check the goddamn
weapon. There were six or seven crates stacked against
the wall near the cockpit door but no cover there, on either side; the thing would have her penned in.

Go go go!

As she scurried along the right wall, the lumbering
creature slowly turning to follow, she grabbed the
semi from under her belt and flicked the safety off by
feel, afraid to look away from it. It stumped toward
her on tree trunk legs, eerily focused on her every
step.

The cargo hold wasn't all that big, maybe thirty-five

feet long and twelve wide. Too soon, she was at the rear of the plane, icy air suddenly pulling at her, working to suck her out into the clouds. Crouching, trying not to think about a misstep, Claire darted across the open space and reached the other wall, grabbing at a raised ridge of metal with trembling fingers.

The creature was still almost twenty feet away. Claire held onto the wall, waiting for it to draw closer before running again. At least it was slow, there was that much, but she had to come up with something, she couldn't keep going around in circles.

She was watching the creature, could see it clearly ... but what happened next was like some optical illusion. It dropped its silvery head slightly—

—and was suddenly five feet away, the distance closed in a fraction of a second, and it was bringing its right arm down, parting the air with an audible *whoosh,* knives flashing—

Claire didn't think, she moved, her stomach suddenly in her throat, her own action a blur to herself. For a split second she was only a body, ducking and sprinting— and then she was on the other side of the plane, all the way up by the stacked crates, looking back as the creature slowly, slowly turned.

Aw, shit on this! The plane would survive a few holes. She opened fire, sent eight 9mm rounds in a tight grouping right at the center of its chest—and all of them hit. She saw the black-rimmed holes open up near where its heart would be if it was human, no blood but moist, dark tissue was exposed, forming spongy lumps around the wounds. The creature stopped in its tracks—and started again in about two seconds, one slow step after another, its focus unchanged.

A stab of panic hit her, *gotta get out of here it's going to kill me, get Steve, another gun maybe—*

No, she couldn't, and it wouldn't help, it would only make things worse. Mr. X had been programmed for a single purpose, to obtain a virus sample; she suspected that this creature was after her specifically, and if she left the hold, the creature would just tear through the hatch, killing her *and* Steve. At least this way, he might have a chance. And 9mm was the heaviest firepower on board—if it could take eight rounds in the chest, another gun wasn't going to make a difference.

Try for a head shot, like the one-armed monster.

She could try, but she had the feeling that something that didn't bleed probably wouldn't go blind, either. Its eyes were strange, perhaps they weren't even used for sight . . . and there was also the fact that they were on a moving plane, one that shook and wavered; without a scope, how was she supposed to target, let alone hit?

All that passed through her mind in about a second and then she was moving again, edging toward the back of the plane once more—afraid to run, afraid to stand still, wondering how long she had before it ran at her again and what she would do then—

—and it lowered its head like it had done before, and again, Claire's body reacted, but an idea was forming, too. She pushed away from the wall and ran *toward* it, angling her path, *if this doesn't work I'm dead—*

—and she felt the chill of its strange flesh as it rocketed past her, was so close that she could smell its rotten meat smell—and then they were on opposite ends of the open space and it was slowly, mechanically turning around. It had worked, but barely; if it had been an inch closer, if she'd been a half step slower, it would already be over.

Guns didn't work, she couldn't leave, so the creature had to go, *but how?* The air stream at the hold's open end was strong, but if *she* could duck past it, no way it would nab the weighty monstrosity . . . she had to knock it off-balance, maybe bait it to the opening and trip it up somehow, she wasn't strong enough to push it . . .

Think, damnit! It was starting toward her again, one step, two. She looked away long enough to scan the floor near the opening, looking for something it might stumble over, maybe the hydraulic track—

The hydraulic track.

Used to push heavy crates to the rear of the plane, to be unloaded. In fact, two of the empty crates were sitting on the metal platform at the start of the track, just a few steps from the door to the cockpit. The controls were set into the outer wall, right in front of the door.

Too slow, there's no way. Except it was slow because it carried a heavy load; if there was only an empty container or two on the platform, how fast would it go then? She had to get to the controls, had to see—

There was a blur of movement, and then the spiked mace was coming around, ripping toward the side of her head. Claire jumped forward, instinctively sidestepped, but not quite fast enough. The spikes didn't get her but its powerful forearm did, bashing painfully into her ear, knocking her off her feet.

Instantly, the creature crouched and brought its right arm down, but she was already in motion, rolling the second she hit the floor. The hand blades hit the deck and sparks flew, the creature howling in rage as Claire sprang to her feet, trying not to notice her throbbing ear or the tiny black dots that swarmed at the edges of her vision. She ran for the hydraulic controls instead, as the creature rose to its feet, its movements mechanical again, as emotionless as it had been furious only seconds before.

A few running steps and she was looking down at a simple control panel, power switch, a dial for entering approximate weight, buttons for back and forth, a tiny readout screen, an emergency shutoff. Claire hit the power switch, twisting the weight dial to the maximum limit, just under three tons.

She shot a look at the creature, still at a safe distance, and saw that it was only a step or two from being in the direct path of the platform. Her hand hovered over the blue switch that would move it forward, that should send it bulleting down the hold at an incredible speed. With only a few pounds of empty container where three tons was expected, it would mow the creature down like a blade of grass.

Almost . . . almost . . . now!

When the creature was standing almost directly on the track, Claire punched the button—and nothing happened, nothing at all.

Shit! She fumbled for the power switch again, maybe she hadn't turned it on—and she saw what was on the little readout screen, and groaned aloud. The simple instructions read, "Charging for load—wait for tone."

Good God, how long will that *be?*

The creature was still twenty feet away, walking almost directly along the track. She might not get a better shot at it, because another blow could very well mean her death—but if she stayed where she was and the creature got to her before the platform was charged, she'd be trapped between the wall and the storage crates. It would bludgeon her into pulp against the cockpit door.

Better to run for it.

Better to stay put.

Claire hesitated a touch too long, and the creature was in motion again. It swept toward her like a natural disaster and it was too late, not even time to turn around and flee into the cockpit—

—ping!

—and it brought its spiked left hand down just as Claire slammed the switch, her eyes squeezed closed, sure that the world was about to disappear in a blizzard of pain—

—as the creature shot away from her, roaring, the empty crates lifting it off its feet, powering it away. Before she could begin to accept that the plan was working, the creature used one of its incredible bursts of speed and got in front of the barreling container, just enough to get some leverage, to push against it—

—but Claire didn't wait to see which force was greater. She opened fire again, two, three bullets hitting it in the head, bouncing harmlessly off its armored skull—but distracting it, too. The creature struggled another half second and then it and the two crates were gone, plunging into the dusky sky.

Claire stared out at the passing stream of atmosphere for a time, knowing she should feel limp with relief—that she'd killed the monster, that she'd survived another Umbrella disaster, that they were finally, *finally* safe . . . but she was simply wrung out, any possibility for strong emotion having flown out the back along with Mr. X's big brother.

"Please, let it be over," she said softly, and then turned and opened the door back into the cockpit.

As she hopped the two steps up to the pilot area, Steve glanced back her, frowning. "What happened? Is everything okay?"

Claire nodded, flopping down in the seat next to him, absolutely beat. "Yeah. Score one more for the good guys. Oh, the rear cargo hatch is gone."

"Are you kidding?" Steve asked.

"Nope," Claire said, and yawned widely, suddenly overwhelmed with fatigue. "Hey, I'm going to rest my eyes for a minute. If I fall asleep, wake me up in five, okay?"

"Sure," Steve said, still looking confused. "The hatch is *gone?*"

Claire didn't answer him, the dark already rushing up to claim her, her body melting into the seat . . .

. . . and then Steve was shaking her, repeating her name over and over again.

"Claire! Claire!"

"Yeah," she mumbled, sure she hadn't slept as she cracked her eyes open, wondering why Steve would want to torture her like this—until she saw his expression, and a bolt of alarm jolted her awake.

"What, what is it?" she asked, sitting up straight.

Steve looked really worried. "Like a minute ago, we changed direction and then the controls suddenly locked down," he said. "I don't know what it is, there's no radio but everything else is still working fine—except I can't steer, or alter altitude or speed. It's like it's stuck on autopilot."

Before she could say a word, there was a crackling static sound from a small video monitor mounted close to the ceiling of the cockpit, one Claire hadn't noticed before. Flickering distortion lines spread out across the screen, but the picture, when it came in, was clear enough.

Alfred!

He was also flying, it seemed, belted into the front seat of a two-man fighter jet, or something similar. He still had smears of makeup on his face, his eyes rimmed in black, and when he spoke, it was in Alexia's voice.

"My apologies," he purred, "but I can't let you escape now. It seems you've eluded another of my playthings—naughty, naughty."

"Cross-dressing freak," Steve snapped, but Alfred either didn't hear him or didn't care.

"Enjoy the ride," Alfred said, giggling, and with a final buzz of static, the screen went blank.

Claire stared at Steve, who stared back helplessly, and then they both looked out over the sea of clouds, watching silently as the first shafts of sunlight broke through.

Steve was dreaming about his father when he started awake suddenly, afraid for some reason, the dream slipping away even as he remembered where he was. Claire made a soft, sleepy sound in the back of her throat and nuzzled closer, her head against his left shoulder, her breath warm against his chest.

Oh, Steve thought, afraid to move, not wanting to wake her up. They'd fallen asleep side-by-side leaning against the cockpit wall, and had apparently moved closer together at some point. He had no idea what time it was, or how long they'd slept, but they were still in the air, muted sunlight still coming in through the windows.

They'd talked for a while after Alfred had taken control of the plane, but not about what they were going to do at the end of their hijacked ride. Claire had remarked that since they couldn't do anything about it, there was no point in worrying. Instead, they'd eaten—Claire had nabbed a few packs of vending machine nuts, for which Steve would be eternally grateful—and done their best to wash up using a little of the bottled water, and then talked. Really talked.

She'd told him about going to Raccoon City to find Chris, and everything that had happened there and what she knew about Umbrella and Trent the spy-guy . . . and she'd told him a lot of other stuff, too. She was in college, and two years older than him, and she rode a motorcycle but was probably going to give it up because of how dangerous it was. She liked to dance so she liked dance music, but she also liked grunge, and she thought politics were mostly boring, and cheeseburgers were her favorite food. She was totally, incredibly cool, the coolest girl he'd ever met—and even better, she'd actually been interested in what *he* had to say. She'd laughed at a lot of his jokes, and thought it was cool that he ran track, and when he'd talked some about his parents, she'd listened without getting all pushy.

And she's so smart, and beautiful . . .

He looked down at her, at her tousled hair and long lashes, his heart pounding even though he was trying to relax. She moved again, shifting in her sleep, her head tilting back a little—and her slightly parted lips were suddenly close enough for him to kiss, all he had to do was tip his face down a few inches, and he wanted to so bad that he actually started to do it, lowering his mouth toward hers—

"Mmmm," she murmured, still totally asleep, and he stopped, pulling back, his heart beating even faster. He totally wanted to but not like that, not if she didn't want him to. He *thought* she did, but she'd also told him a little about her friend Leon, too, and he wasn't so sure that they were just friends.

Feeling tortured, having her so close but not his, he was relieved when she rolled away from him a few seconds later. He stood up, stretching stiff legs, and walked to the front of the plane, wondering if the reserve fuel tank had been tapped yet, the thought of dealing with that crazy Ashford asshole once again drying up the last of his positive feelings. He hoped that Claire would sleep awhile longer, she'd been so tired—

—until he saw what was outside, and read the heading, and realized that their altitude had dropped considerably. The plane was starting to pitch some, bucking, and no wonder. On the map reader next to the compass was an approximate latitude-longitude for their position.

"Claire, wake up! You gotta come see this!"

A few seconds later she was at his side, rubbing her eyes—which widened considerably when she looked out the window. There was a near blizzard of ice and snow pounding down, extending as far as they could see.

"We're over the Antarctic," Steve said.

"As in the South Pole?" Claire asked, incredulous. She grabbed the back of the copilot seat as the plane roller-coastered. "Penguins and killer whales, all that?"

"I don't know about the wildlife, but we're at a latitude of 82.17 South," Steve said. "Definitely the bottom of the world. And I'm not positive, but I think we're coming in for a landing. We're slowing down, anyway."

Maybe Alfred's plan was to drop them in the middle of nowhere and let them freeze to death. Not flashy, but it would certainly do the trick. Steve wished he could get his bare hands on the guy for just a minute, just one. He wasn't much of a fighter, but Alfred would melt like a cream puff.

"We must be headed for that," Claire said, pointing right, and Steve squinted, barely able to see through the storm . . . and then he saw the other planes, and the long, low buildings that she had spotted, only a few minutes away.

"You think it's one of Umbrella's?" Steve asked, knowing before she nodded that it had to be. Where else?

The plane's nose continued to dip down, carrying them to whatever Alfred had in mind, but Steve was actually a little relieved. Meeting up with Umbrella again sucked, of course, but at least someone else would be in charge, and not every Umbrella employee was as shrink-wrapped as Alfred. He couldn't imagine that everyone would drop what they were doing to kiss Alfred's ass, either. Maybe he and Claire could find someone to bargain with, or bribe somehow . . .

They were closing in for a first pass, the ride getting squirrelly, the wings probably heavy with ice—when Steve realized that they were way too low, too low and too fast. The landing gear had dropped at some point, but there was no way they could land at their speed and altitude.

"Pull up, pull up . . . " Steve said, watching the buildings get big too quickly, feeling prickles of sweat breaking out all over. He slid into the pilot's chair, grabbing the yoke and pulling back—and nothing happened.

Oh, man.

"Belt up, we're going to crash!" Steve shouted, grabbing for his own belt as Claire jumped into her seat, the buckles snapping shut just as they touched down—

—and alarms started shrieking as the landing gear crumpled and tore away, the plane's belly slamming into the ground. The cabin bounced wildly, the seat belts the only thing keeping them from hitting the roof. Claire let out a yelp as a wave of snow crashed into the windshield, and there was a giant metal *SCREECH* behind them as the tail or a wing ripped away—

—and enough of the churning snow pack fell away from the glass for them to see the building in front of them, the out of control plane sliding for it, smoke coming from somewhere, they were going to hit and—

†ᴇᴨ

CLAIRE'S HEAD HURT. AGAIN.

Something was on fire, she could smell smoke and she was incredibly cold, and she suddenly remembered what had happened—the snow, the building, the crash. Alfred. She opened her eyes and lifted her head, the action awkward and difficult because she was still strapped into her chair, now tilted forward at about a 45 degree angle—and there was Steve in his chair, not moving.

"Steve! Steve, wake up!"

Steve groaned and mumbled something, and Claire breathed easier. After a few tries she managed to get her belt off and slid into a crouch, her feet on what had been the instrument panel. She couldn't see much out of the windshield with the angle they were at, but it appeared that they were inside some big building. There was gray metal siding some fifty or sixty feet in front of them, and through the gaping hole on her side of the plane, she could see a bit of walkway with a railing maybe eight or nine feet below.

So where is everybody? Where is anybody? If it *was* an Umbrella facility, why weren't there a dozen soldiers dragging them out of the wreckage? Or at least a few pissed off janitors . . .

Steve was coming around, though she could see a nasty bump at the edge of his hairline. She reached up and found that she had a matching bump just above her right temple, about an inch higher than the one she'd woken up with . . . yesterday? The day before?

My, how time flies when you keep getting knocked unconscious.

"What's burning?" Steve asked, opening bleary eyes.

"I don't know," Claire said. There was just a trace of smoke in the cabin, she figured it was coming from some other part of the plane. In any case, she didn't want to stick around, see if anything blew up. "But we should get out of here. Do you think you can walk?"

"These boots were *made* for walking," Steve mumbled, and Claire grinned, helping him with his belt.

They salvaged what they could from the weaponry that was piled at their feet, Steve's machine pistol and her 9mm. Unfortunately, they were low on ammo, and a couple of clips had gone missing. She had twenty-seven rounds, he had fifteen. They split them up, and with nothing else to keep them aboard, Steve lowered himself out over the walkway, dropping the last few feet.

"What's out there?" Claire asked, sitting on the edge of the hole and tucking her gun in her belt. It was cold enough for her to see her breath, but she thought she could manage for a little while.

"Not a whole hell of a lot," Steve called back, looking around. "We're in a big round building—I think it's built around a mine shaft or something, there's a straight drop through the middle. There's nobody here."

He looked up at her and raised his arms. "Come on down, I gotcha."

Claire doubted it. He was in good shape but had a runner's physique, not overly muscular. On the other hand, she couldn't stay in the plane all day, and she hated jumping off things higher than a few feet, she definitely wanted a helping hand . . .

"Coming down," she said, and pushed herself off the hole's edge, holding on as long she could—

—and then she was dropping, and Steve emitted an "oof" sound, and then they were both on the ground, Steve on his back with his arms around her, Claire on top of him.

"Nice catch," she said.

"Aw, 'twarn't nothin'," Steve said, smiling.

He was warm. And attractive, and sweet, and obviously interested, and for a few seconds, neither of them moved, Claire content to be held . . . and Steve wanting more, she could see it in the way he searched her face.

For Christ's sake, you're not on a vacation! Move!

"We should probably . . ."

" . . . figure out where we are," Steve finished, and though she could see a flash of disappointment in his eyes, he did his best to hide it, sighing melodramatically as he dropped his arms in pretend surrender. Reluctantly, she got to her feet and helped him to his.

It did seem to be a mine shaft, sixty feet across give or take, the walkway they were on running about half way around, in steps—there were a couple of ladders, and she could see at least two doors from where they were, all down and to their left. There was only one door on their level, to the right, but Steve checked and it was locked.

"So where do you think everybody is?" he asked, keeping his voice low. There was a definite echo effect probability, as massive and empty as the chamber was.

Claire shook her head. "Making snow angels?"

"Ha ha," Steve said. "Shouldn't Alfred be jumping out right about now with a flame thrower or something?"

"Yeah, probably," Claire said. She'd been thinking that herself. "Maybe he isn't here yet, or he didn't expect us to crash, so he's in one of the other buildings where we were supposed to land . . . which means we should book. If we can get to one of those other planes before he finds us . . ."

"Let's do it," Steve said. "Do you want to split up? We could cover more ground that way, hurry things along."

"With Alfred running around somewhere? I vote no," Claire said, and Steve nodded, looking relieved.

"So . . . thataway," Claire said, and started for the first ladder, Steve right behind.

A short climb later and they were at the next door to try, actually double doors set in a little ways from the walkway. Also locked. Steve offered to try and kick it in, but she suggested they try the others first. She was feeling more and more uneasy about how quiet things were, and didn't want the echoing thunder of a door being broken down to announce their presence, *though they'd have to be comatose not to have heard or felt the crash . . .*

On to the next, the only other door before an opening in the wall with a flight of stairs going down. Claire jiggled the handle and it turned easily; she and Steve readied their weapons just in case—and at a nod from Steve, Claire pushed the door open—

—and felt her mouth drop open, totally shocked.

What are the odds on that?

It was a bunk room, dark and reeking, and at the sound of the door opening, three, four zombies turned and started for them, all of them freshly infected, most of their skin still attached. At least one of them was starting to go gangrenous, the noxious smell of hot, rotting tissue heavy in the cold air.

Steve had gone pale, and as she slammed the door closed, he swallowed, hard, looking and sounding kind of sick. "One of those guys worked at Rockfort. He was a cook."

Of course! She'd thought for a second that there'd been a spill here, too, but that really was too giant of a coincidence. At least one of those planes outside had come from the island, probably a bunch of panicked employees—presumably not scientists—who hadn't realized they were carrying the infection with them.

More sick and dying viral cannibals . . . and what else? Claire shuddered, trying to imagine the kind of soldier Umbrella would be trying to invent for an arctic environment . . . and what natural animals might have been infected before their arrival.

"We definitely gotta get out of here," Steve said.

Well, maybe Alfred got eaten, anyway, Claire thought. Wishful thinking, though they certainly deserved a lucky break. "Let's go."

The last place to check, a set of winding stairs, marked the end of the walkway, descending into a near total darkness. Remembering the matches she'd found at Rockfort, Claire handed Steve her gun and fished them out of her pack, giving him half before taking her weapon back. He took the lead, striking two of the matches about halfway down the stairs and holding them up. They didn't give off much light, but they were better than nothing.

They reached the bottom and started to edge forward down a tight hall, Claire on high alert as the darkness closed around them. Something smelled bad, like rotting grain, and though she couldn't hear anything moving, it didn't feel like they were alone. She was generally big on trusting her instincts, but it was so still and silent, not even a whisper of sound or movement . . .

Nerves, she thought hopefully.

They could only see about three feet in front of them, but they moved as quickly as possible, the feeling of being totally exposed and vulnerable pushing them forward.

A few steps more and she could see that the corridor branched, they could keep going straight or turn left.

"What do you think?" Claire whispered—and the hall suddenly exploded with movement, wings flapping, the rotten smell gusting over them. Steve cursed as the matches suddenly went out, completing the darkness. Something brushed past Claire's face, feathery and light and soundless, and she reflexively flailed at it in loathing, skin crawling, not sure where or what to shoot.

"Come on!" Steve shouted, grabbing her upper arm and yanking her forward. She stumbled after him breathlessly, and again, something fluttering touched her face, dry and dusty—

—and then Steve was pulling her through a doorway and slamming it closed behind them, both of them sagging against it, Claire shuddering, totally disgusted.

"Moths," Steve said, "Jesus, they were huge, did you see them? Big as birds, like hawks—" She could hear him spit, like he was trying to clear his mouth out.

Claire didn't answer, fumbling for a match. The room was pitch dark and she wanted to make sure there weren't more of them flapping around, *moths, eeww!* They somehow seemed worse than any zombie, that they could brush right up against you, flutter up against your face—she shuddered again, and struck her match.

Steve had pulled them into an office, one apparently free of giant moths and any other Umbrella unpleasantness. She saw a pair of candlesticks on a trunk to her right and immediately grabbed them up, lighting the half burned tapers and handing one of them to Steve before looking around, the soft candlelight illuminating their sanctuary in flickering shadows. Wood desk, shelves, a couple of framed paintings—the room was surprisingly nice, considering the utilitarian feel of the rest of the place. It wasn't as cold, either. They quickly checked around for weapons or ammo, but came up empty.

"Hey, maybe there's something we can use in these," Steve said, moving to the desk. There were a number of papers, and what appeared to be a collection of maps

strewn across its top—but Claire was suddenly more interested in the whitish lump stuck on the back of his
right shoulder.

"Hold still," she said, stepping up behind him.
There was some thick, web-like gunk holding the
thing on, the lump itself about six inches long and
kind of misshapen, like a chicken egg that had been
stretched out.

"What is it? Get it off," Steve said tensely, and Claire
held the candle closer, saw that the white form wasn't
entirely opaque. She could see inside, a little . . .

. . . to where a fat white grub was squirming around,
encased in translucent jelly. It was an egg case, the moth
had laid an *egg case* on him.

Claire wanted to vomit but held it together, looking
around for something to grab it with. There was some
crumpled paper in a wastebasket next to the trunk, and
she snatched up a piece.

"Hang on a sec," she said, amazed at how casual she
sounded as she pulled the case off his shoulder. It didn't
want to come, the wet webbing tenaciously holding on,
but she got it, instantly dropping it to the floor. "It's off."

Steve turned and crouched next to the paper, holding
his candle out—and stood up abruptly, looking as sickened as she felt. He brought his boot down on it, hard,
and clear jelly squirted from beneath the sole.

"Oh, man," he said, his mouth turned down. "Remind
me to blow chunks later, after we've eaten. And next
time we go through there, no matches."

He checked her back—clean, thank God—and then
they split up the papers on the desk, Steve taking the

maps and sitting on the floor, Claire looking through the rest of it at the desk.

Inventory list, bill, bill, list . . . Claire hoped Steve was having better luck. From what she could gather, they were in what Umbrella was calling a "transport terminal," whatever that was, and it had been built around an abandoned mine—she wasn't clear on what had been mined, exactly, but there were a number of receipts for some newer spendy equipment and a shitload of construction materials. Almost enough to build a small city.

She found a series of memos between two extremely boring gentlemen, discussing Umbrella's budget allotments for the coming year. It was all the more boring because everything appeared to be perfectly legal. The office they were in belonged to one of them, a Tomoko Oda, and it was from Oda that she finally ran across something that caught her eye, a postscript on one of his lengthy accounting reports dated from only a week before.

PS—by the way, remember the story you told me when I first got here, about the "monster" prisoner? Don't laugh, but I finally heard him myself, two nights ago, in this very office. It was just as frightening as the stories say, a kind of angry, moaning scream that echoed up from the lower levels. My foreman tells me that workers have been hearing it for something like 15 years, almost always late at night—the most popular rumor has it that he screams like that because someone missed his feeding time. I've also heard that he's a ghost, a hoax, a scientific experiment gone wrong, even a demon. I haven't formed an opinion myself, and since none of us are allowed down there, I suppose it will continue to be a mystery. I have to tell you, though, after hearing that horrible, insane howling, I have no interest in going below B2.

Let me know about that stem bolt shipment. Regards, Tom.

It seemed that the workers upstairs didn't know much about what was going on downstairs. Probably better for them, Claire thought . . . although considering the current situation, maybe not.

Steve laughed suddenly, a short bark of victory, and stood up, grinning widely. He slapped an Antarctica political map across the desk.

"We're here," Steve said, pointing to a red spot that someone had penciled in, "about halfway in between this Japanese outpost, Dome Fuji, and the Pole itself, in the Australian territory. And right *here* is an Australian research station—we're looking at ten or fifteen miles, tops."

Claire felt her heart skip a beat. "That's great! Hell, we could probably hike it if we could find some good gear . . ."

. . . and if we can get out of this basement, she thought, some of her enthusiasm dying down.

Steve unfolded a second map, spreading it out. "Wait, that's not the good part. Check this out."

A photocopy of a blueprint. Claire studied the hand-drawn diagrams, side and top views of a tall building and three of its floors, the levels and rooms neatly labeled—and stood up herself, too elated to stay still. It was a comprehensive map of the building they were in, not tall but deep.

"This is where we are at now," Steve said, pointing to a small square labeled "manager's office," on level B2. He traced his finger down and left and down again, stopping at an oddly shaped area at the bottom of the diagram, like a big quotation mark lying on its side. The tiny black letters read "mining room," and there was a lightly penciled tunnel extending out of it with "to surface/unfinished" written next to it, also in pencil.

"And there's where we need to go," Claire finished, shaking her head in disbelief. The map Steve had found would probably save them hours of wandering around, and with as little ammo as they had, it might also save their lives.

"Yeah. If we run into any locked doors, we break 'em down, or shoot the locks, maybe," Steve said happily. "And it's like a one-minute walk from here. We'll be flying the friendly skies in no time."

"It says the tunnel is unfinished—" Claire started, but Steve cut her off.

"So? If they're still working on it, there'll be some kind of equipment laying around," Steve said happily. "I mean, it says mining room, right?"

She couldn't argue with his logic, and didn't want to. It was almost too good to be true, and she was more than ready for some good news . . . and though it *did* mean another run through mothville, this time, they'd be ready.

"You win the prize," Claire said, giving in to her own enthusiasm.

Steve raised his eyebrows innocently. "Oh, yeah? What's the prize?"

She was about to answer that she was open to suggestions when an unexpected and alarming noise stopped her, coming into the office from nowhere and everywhere. For a split second she thought it was some kind of an air raid siren, it was so loud and penetrating, but no siren started so deep and low, or kept rising like that, or conjured up such feelings of dread. There was fury in the sound, a blind rage so complete that it was incomprehensible.

Frozen, they listened as the incredible, grisly scream stretched out and finally died away, Claire wondering how long it had been since feeding time. She had no doubt that it was one of Umbrella's creations. No ghost could produce such a visceral sound, and no human soul could encompass such rage.

"Let's go now," Claire said quietly, and Steve nodded, his eyes wide and anxious as he folded the maps and tucked them away.

They readied their weapons, laid out a quick plan, and on the count of three, Steve shoved the door open.

As the monstrosity's roar echoed away, Alfred smiled at it through the thick metal bars of its bare, dank cell, admiring his sister's handiwork. He'd helped, of course, but she was the genius who'd created the T-Veronica virus, and at only ten years of age . . . and though she had considered her first experiment a failure, Alfred thought not. The result was deeply gratifying on a personal level.

Things were so much clearer, had been since the very moment he'd left Rockfort. Memories had returned, things he'd buried or lost, feelings he'd forgotten he had. After fifteen years of gray area, of muddled confusion and unstable fantasy, Alfred felt that his world was finally drawing to order—and he understood now why their home had been attacked, and how fortunate for him that it had been.

"They knew that it was time, too, you see," Alfred said. "If not for the strike, I might have continued to believe that she was with me."

He watched with some amusement as the monstrosity tilted its filthy head toward the door, listening. It was chained to its chair, blindfolded, hands bound behind its back . . . and though it had been incapable of anything like real thought for a decade and a half, it still responded to the sound of words. Perhaps it even recognized his voice on some animal instinctual level.

I should feed it, Alfred thought, not wanting it to die before Alexia awoke . . . but that would be soon, very soon—perhaps the process had already begun. The thought filled him with wonder, that he was to be present for her miraculous rebirth.

"I missed her so," Alfred said, sighing. So much that he'd created a reflection of her, to share the lonely years of waiting. "But she's soon to emerge a reigning queen, with me as her faithful soldier, and we'll never be apart again."

Which reminded him of his final task, a last objective

to be met before he could comfortably begin the final wait. His joy at discovering the crashed plane had been short-lived when he'd found it empty, but upon refreshing himself of the terminal's layout, he'd realized the peasant couple could only be in one or two places. He'd taken a sniper rifle from the armory at one of the other buildings, a 30.06 bolt action Remington with a magnifying scope, a delightful toy, and was determined to try it out. He couldn't have Claire and her little friend showing up at some inopportune moment, mangling the celebration—

Suddenly, Alfred started to laugh, a gem of an idea occurring to him. The monstrosity had to eat . . . why not bring it the two commoners? Claire Redfield had brought destruction down upon Rockfort, had attempted to soil the Ashford name, just as the monstrosity had, in a way.

It will consume the enemy agents, an observance in honor of Alexia's return . . . and then we'll have a private family reunion, just the three of us.

At the sound of his laughter, the monstrosity became agitated, pulling at its chains with such force that Alfred stopped laughing. It let out another tremendous, lingering roar, straining to be free, but Alfred thought the restraints would hold a bit longer.

"I'll be back soon," Alfred promised, hefting his rifle and walking away, wondering what Claire would think about meeting his and Alexia's father under such unusual circumstances—namely, her own bloody death. The monstrosity was drawn to body heat and the smell of terror, Alfred liked to believe, very much looking forward to watching a helpless Claire stalked through the dark.

As Alfred started up the stairs to the second basement level, Alexander Ashford screamed again, as he'd done fifteen years before when his own children had drugged him and stolen his life.

ELEVEⁿ

THEY PUSHED OUT INTO THE DARK, STEVE ahead of Claire, leaving the office door open. There was just enough light to see where the hall branched right, which was all the light they needed.

*—right, walk, door on the right, walk, steps to the left—*It looped through his mind, the directions simple but he didn't want to make even a tiny mistake. The image of what Claire had pulled off his back was still fresh in his mind, and they didn't know what else the moths could do.

Two strides forward and the first moth came at them, a whitish, silent blur, and Steve opened up.

Bam-bam-bam! Three shots and the flapping thing disintegrated, soft *plop* sounds as the pieces hit the floor, and here came the rest, fluttering out from the corridor he and Claire wanted. They flew on a dusty wave of rot smell, shadowy, flopping shapes . . . and what was that, the thick, hanging, man-size thing webbed against the ceiling?

—don't think about it, now, go now—

"Now!" Steve said, and Claire ran out from behind him, darting to the right and down the hall as he opened fire again, two- and three-round bursts.

Feathery pieces of wing and warm, repulsive goo rained down as he fired into the whirling dark shapes overhead, splashing him, making him gag, the moths dying as silently as they attacked. He felt one of them in his hair, felt something warm and wet touch his scalp, and frantically brushed at the top of his head, firing, knocking a sticky egg case away.

"Open!" Claire shouted, much closer than he expected, and though he'd planned to back down the hall, firing as he went, the feel of that crap in his hair was the last straw. He ducked, covered his head with one arm, and sprinted.

He saw her silhouette in a doorway on the right and plunged ahead, running directly into her outstretched arm. Claire grabbed a handful of his shirt and jerked him inside, slamming the door closed behind them—and then turned and started firing, blocking his body with hers.

"Hey, what's—"

Bam! Bam! The room was huge, the shots echoing from faraway corners.

There was a trace of light coming from somewhere, but Steve heard them before he saw them. Zombies, moaning and gasping, three or four of them closing in on their position. He could only make out their outlines, staggering and weaving forward, saw two of them go down but two more moving in to take their place.

"I'm okay!" he called out between rounds, and Claire stepped aside, shouting for him to take the right flank.

Steve targeted and fired, blinking and squinting against the dark, trying to get head shots. He took down three of them, then a fourth, so close that he felt blood splashing his hand. He immediately wiped it against his pants, praying that he didn't have any open cuts, that he wouldn't run out of ammo, but there was another zombie, and another—

—and then Claire was pulling him again and he stopped firing, let her lead him through the dark toward where the mining room was supposed to be. Behind them, zombies shuffled and wailed, giving slow motion chase. He tripped over a warm body and stepped on another, feeling something crunch underfoot—but as helpless and afraid as he felt, it was nothing to suddenly hearing Claire cry out in pain, to feel her fingers leave his arm.

"Claire!" Terrified, Steve reached out for her, felt only air—

"Watch your step, I stubbed my goddamn toe," Claire said irritably, no more than two feet away, and he felt his knees go weak. He could also feel a cold metal railing against his right shoulder—the steps to the mining room. They'd made it.

Together, they climbed the few steps, Claire still in front—and when she opened the door, real light spilled out in shafts, piercing the blackness.

"Praise Jesus," Steve muttered, holding the door from behind as Claire stepped inside—

—and before he could follow, he heard that disturbed, girlish giggling that he'd come to know and hate, and

Claire had slipped one hand behind her back and was motioning him to freeze. He let go of the door and she didn't move, letting it settle on her hip as Alfred said something and she slowly raised both her hands.

It seemed Alfred had gotten the drop on Claire . . .

. . . *but not on me,* Steve thought, unaware that he was wearing a tight, grim smile. Alfred had a lot to answer for, but Steve was pretty certain that in another minute or two, he wasn't going to be saying much of anything, ever again.

He had her. As he'd surmised, they—well, *she* had come to see about the tunnel, the one exit from the terminal that didn't require a key. She wasn't a stupid girl, by no means, but he was superior, in intellect and strategy. Among other things.

Still standing in the doorway, Claire raised her hands, her expression annoyingly blank. Why wasn't she afraid?

"Drop your weapon," Alfred snapped, his finger on the rifle's trigger. His voice, naturally amplified by the mining pit that took up most of the floor, emanated throughout the icy chamber, sounding authoritative and a bit cruel. He liked the strong sound of it, and knew it was effective when she let the handgun drop from her fingers without hesitating.

"Kick it toward me," he commanded, and she did so, the weapon clattering across the concrete. He didn't pick it up, instead kicking it beneath the rail to his left, both of them listening to her only hope bounce away over frozen rocks, lost to the depths of the icy pit.

How wonderful, to exert such control!

"What happened to your traveling companion?" he asked, sneering. "Has he met with an accident? Oh, and step away from the door, if you don't mind. And keep your hands when I can see them."

Claire edged forward, the door mostly closing behind her, and he saw a flash of some unhappy emotion cross her face, knew immediately that he'd scored a point. Less of a hot meal for father, it seemed, but he doubted the monstrosity would complain.

"He's dead," she said simply. "What happened to Alexia? Or am I speaking to Alexia—you know, you two look so much alike . . ."

"Shut your mouth, little girl," Alfred snarled. "You don't deserve to say her name. You already know that it's time for her return, that's why your people attacked Rockfort, to lure her out—or were you hoping to kill her outright, to cut short her first breath?"

Claire acted confused, determined to keep up her pretense, it seemed, but Alfred didn't want to hear any more of her lies. The game was losing interest for him. In the face of Alexia's imminent triumph, everything had paled by comparison.

"I already know it all," he snapped, "so don't bother. Now, if you'll come with me—"

Claire suddenly looked up and right, to the raised platform where the tunnel began.

"Look out!" she shrieked, collapsing as Alfred spun around, seeing only the massive ice digger machine, the tunnel's dark entrance—

—and the door had crashed open behind Claire, the

boy diving in and landing on his side, pointing a weapon at him, at *him*.

Furious, Alfred swung the rifle and pulled the trigger, three, four times, but he hadn't had enough time to target properly, the explosive shots going wide—

—and it was as though a giant hand suddenly shoved Alfred backward, taking his breath away, the boy firing and then clicking on empty, out of bullets.

Alfred stumbled back another step and opened his mouth to laugh, ready to kill them both and, and the rifle wasn't in his hands anymore, he'd dropped it for some reason, and his laugh was only a wet, painful cough—

—and something gave way behind his back, and then he was falling into the mining pit. He landed on a thick crust of ice and started to get up, but there was a great, searing pain in his chest. Was it possible that he'd been *shot?*

With barely a sound, the ice gave way all around him and he screamed, falling, he had to see her once more, had to touch her but he could hear his father screaming, too, coming for him, and then everything was lost in pain and dark.

The sound of the terrible, monstrous howl that had risen up to meet Alfred's got them moving, Claire pausing just long enough to grab the Remington before climbing after Steve to the high platform. With Steve on empty and her own gun kicked into the pit, it was their only weapon.

They clambered into the cab of the huge yellow machine parked in front of the slanted, rising tunnel, Steve taking the wheel—and again, they heard that deep, insane scream, and it was definitely closer, the monster prisoner loose somewhere inside.

Steve flipped a bunch of switches, nodding and mumbling to himself as he went. Claire listened as she checked the rifle—only six rounds—gathering that the machine's digging device, an enormous screw-looking thing, actually heated up to melt the ice. She didn't care what it did, as long as it got them out before the monster came looking for them.

With the heavy machine humming to life, Steve explained that the tunnel was probably unfinished because the workers would have had to go slowly and without using the heating element, to avoid flooding half the facility.

"But we don't," he said, grinning. "What do you say we make a lake?"

"Go for it," she said, grinning back at him, wishing she felt a little more enthusiastic. God, they were getting out, and with Alfred Ashford finally dead, there was no one standing in their way. So why was she still so uncertain?

It's that shit he was babbling about his sister . . . Crazy, yeah, but it had brought up the one question she still didn't have an answer for—why had Rockfort been attacked?

Steve jammed on the throttle and the machine lurched forward. There weren't seat belts, so Claire put one hand on the roof, the digger bouncing almost as much as their plane had right before it crashed. Their view was mostly blocked by the giant twisting screw-thing, but it was obvious when they hit the end of the tunnel, big-time.

The noise was incredible, deafening, like rocks in a blender times a hundred. There was a burning steam smell, and as they inched forward through total blackness, she could hear the thaw even over the digging, as torrents of water rushed past the cab.

The grinding, waterfall noises seemed to go on forever as they continued to climb—and then the machine stuttered, jerking, and the treads were straining—and sudden light flooded into the cab, gray and shadowy and beautiful.

The digger crawled out of its brand-new hole near a standing tower, Claire recognizing it as a helipad even as Steve pointed out the snow-cats parked near the base. It was snowing, fat wet flakes spinning down from a slate sky, the humid cold seeping into the cab before they'd been on the surface a minute. There was a wind blowing, the snow angled slightly—not a big wind, but steady.

" 'Copter or 'cat?" Steve asked lightly, but she could see that he was starting to shiver. So was she.

"Your call, fly boy," she said. A helicopter would be faster, but staying on the ground seemed safer. "Can we even take off in this?"

"As long as it doesn't get any worse," he said, looking up at the tower, but he didn't seem sure. She was about to recommend one of the 'cats when he shrugged, pushing his door open and sliding out, calling back over his shoulder.

"I say we hit the tower, fly girl," he said. "We can at least see if there's actually a choice."

She got out, too, craning her neck back, but she

couldn't see the top of the tower, either. And it was cold, frostbite cold.

"Whatever, let's just hurry," Claire said, slinging the rifle over her shoulder.

Steve jogged for the stairs, Claire following, freezing but exhilarated, suddenly totally high on being free to choose, to decide what they wanted to do, how they wanted to do it. And either way, they'd be at the Australian station in an hour or so, wrapped in blankets and drinking something hot and telling their story.

Well, at least the more believable parts, she thought, climbing the recently sanded stairs after him. Even the most open-minded people in the world wouldn't believe half of what they'd been through.

Her happiness was wearing thin as they neared the top, three stories later, her teeth chattering it away—and when Steve turned around, frowning, she no longer cared about much of anything beyond getting warm.

"There's no helicopter," he said, snow starting to stick to his hair. "I guess we'll—"

He saw something behind her and his face suddenly contorted with horror and surprise. He reached out to pull her up but she was already moving.

"Go!" she said, and he turned and bolted up the stairs, Claire barely a half step behind him. She didn't know what he'd seen—

—*yes you do*—

—but from the look on his face, she knew she didn't want it behind her.

It's the thing, the monster, it was loose and now it's coming for you, her fear helpfully provided, and then

Steve was grabbing her arm and jerking her up the last few steps. She stumbled onto a giant, empty, square platform, the landing lines mostly obscured by fresh snow, a gray haze of anomalous fog making it hard to see clearly.

"Give me the rifle," he breathed, and she ignored him, turned to see if it was true, if she would recognize the awful pain of the thing that had screamed so horribly—

—and as it gained the platform, she saw that it was true, and she recognized it with no trouble at all. She unslung the rifle and backed away, motioning for Steve to stay behind her.

Alfred woke up in a world of pain. He could barely breathe, and there was blood on his face and in his nose and mouth, and when he tried to move, the agony was instant and overwhelming. Every inch of him was broken, cut or smashed or punctured, and he knew he was going to die. All that was left was his surrender to the dark. He was very afraid, but he ached so badly that perhaps sleep would be best . . .

. . . *Alexia* . . .

He couldn't give up, not when he'd been so close— not when he was still so close. He forced his eyes to open, and saw through a thin red haze that he was on one of the lower level platforms that jutted out into the mining pit. He'd fallen at least three levels, perhaps as many as five.

"Aa, lexii-aa," he whispered, and felt blood bubbling up from his chest, felt bones grinding as he shifted, felt afraid of the pain he'd have to endure—but he would go to her, because she was his heart, his great love, and he would be sustained by his name on her lips.

"Give me the rifle," Steve said again, watching the thing take its first stumbling step in their direction, but Claire wasn't listening. She had her eye to the scope, was seeing what he saw but under magnification—and what he saw was an abomination.

Blindfolded, its hands tied behind its back, wearing only a shapeless and stained cut of leather knotted around its waist, the thing had suffered horribly, that much was clear; he could see the raised scars, the ancient welts, bloody shackle marks around its ankles. It looked almost human, but for its oversized body and strange flesh—gray and mottled, sitting over lean muscles that had ruptured through in places, exposing raw tissue. Its torso was bare, and he could see a kind of pulsing redness in the center of its chest, a clear target— and for a few seconds, Steve thought they were safe after all, *it doesn't have any weapons*—

—and there was a splintering, cracking sound, and four asymmetrical appendages, like the jointed legs of an insect, unfolded from its back and upper body, the longest easily ten feet, curling from its right shoulder like a scorpion's tail. It reeled forward another step— and some dark liquid was spraying from its body, from its chest or back. As the droplets struck the frozen cement, a thick, purplish-green gas began to hiss upward from where they landed, blown by the snowy wind first one direction, then another.

It rumbled out some heavy, wordless sound and took another step toward them, the new arms whipping around its hairless head, making it weave from side to side. It could barely keep its balance, and as the thought occurred to him, Steve was already running.

Go in low, head down, knock it off while it's still at the edge—

"Steve!" Claire screamed fearfully, but he was almost there, close enough for the acrid tinge of its self-produced gas to sear his nostrils, *has to be poison, gotta keep it away from her—*

—and just before he rammed into it, something viciously shoved him, slammed into his back and pushed, sending him flying to the ground.

"Steve!" Claire screamed again, this time in absolute horror, because he was skidding across the icy cement on his side, and though he tried to stop himself, scrabbling at the frozen platform with frozen fingers, there was suddenly no platform left.

Steve was only a few feet from the monster when its strange arm whipped down over them both, hitting Steve in the back and hurtling him to the side.

"Steve!"

Steve skipped across the frozen platform like a flat stone on water and disappeared over the edge.

Oh, my God, no!

Claire doubled over, the emotional pain hitting her like a physical blow, sharp and hard in her gut. He'd been trying to protect her, and it had cost him his life.

For a second, she couldn't move or breathe, couldn't feel the cold, didn't care about the monster.

But only for a second.

She looked at the stumbling, tortured animal staggering toward her, knew without doubt that the fury they'd heard came from long, hard years of abuse, of experimentation, and felt nothing. Her heart had sealed itself up, her mind suddenly colder than her body. She straightened, jacking a round into the chamber of the rifle, appraising the situation with a clear eye.

Obviously, she could outrun it, leave it on the platform and be a mile away before it found its way back down—but that wasn't an option, not anymore. Its death would be a mercy, but that didn't figure in to her calculations, either.

It killed Steve, and now I'm going to kill it, she thought coolly, and walked to the northwest corner of the platform, the farthest from the stairs. Its appendages flailing over its head, the monster wove around in a painfully slow half circle, its blind face finally turned in her direction.

It let out another deep, gasping, mindless sound and its body vomited out more of that smoking liquid, some kind of acid or poison, probably. She wondered who had created such a thing, and how—this was no T-virus zombie, and from its abused and tormented state, it wasn't a BOW, either. She supposed she'd never know.

Claire raised the rifle and looked through the scope, focusing in on the pulsating tissue in the center of its chest, then raising to target its blank gray face. She didn't know about the tissue mass at its heart, but she was sure it wouldn't survive a head shot by a 30.06. She didn't want to waste time stalking it, or inflicting unnecessary pain; she just wanted it dead.

She aimed at the center of its forehead. It had a strong jaw and fine, straight nose beneath the puckered flesh, as though it had once been handsome, even aristocratic.

Maybe it's another Ashford, she thought mockingly, and fired.

The monster's head split apart, almost seemed to shatter as the round found its mark. Shards of bone and brain matter flew, all of it as gray as the gray sky, steam rising up from the broken bowl of its skull as it fell—first to its knees, the mutant arms spasming in the snowy air, then onto its ruined face.

Claire felt nothing, no pleasure, no dismay, not even pity. It was dead, that was all, and it was time for her to go. She still didn't feel the cold, but her body was shaking violently, her teeth rattling, and she knew she had to get warm—

"Claire?"

The voice was weak and shuddering and unmistakably Steve's, coming from the platform's east edge. Claire stared at the empty space for a split second, entirely dumbfounded—and then ran, dropping to her hands and knees beneath the soft patter of snow, leaning out to see him awkwardly wrapped around a support post, clinging to the frozen metal with both arms and one leg.

His face was almost blue with cold, but when he saw her, his eyes lit up, a look of incredible relief crossing his pale features.

"You're alive," he said.

"That's my line," she answered, dropping the rifle and bracing herself against the edge, leaning down to grab his arm. It was a struggle, but in another moment, Steve was back on the platform, and then they were on their knees, embracing, too cold to do anything but hang on.

"I'm so sorry, Claire," he said miserably, his face buried in her shoulder. "I couldn't stop it."

Her heart had unsealed when she'd seen him alive, and now tightened painfully. He was all of seventeen years old, his whole life ripped apart by Umbrella, and he'd just very nearly died trying to save her life. Again. And he was *sorry*.

"Don't worry, I got it this time," she said, determined not to cry. "You get the next one, okay?"

Steve nodded, sitting back on his heels to look at her. "I *will*," he said, so vehemently that she had to smile.

"Cool," she said, and crawled to her feet, reaching down to help him up. "That'll save me some work. Now let's go catch a 'cat, yes?"

Supporting each other and staying close for warmth, they made their way to the stairs, neither of them willing to let go.

†WELVE

ALEXIA ASHFORD WATCHED HER TWIN DIE AT her feet, bleeding and in great pain, reaching out to touch the stasis tank with adoration in his dying eyes. He'd never been particularly bright or competent, but she had loved him, very much. His death was a great sadness . . . but also the sign she'd been waiting for. It was time to come out.

She'd known for some months that the end would be soon—or rather the beginning, the emergence of a new life on Earth. Her stasis had remained stable for most of the fifteen years she'd needed, her mind and body unaware of life—unaware that she was suspended in freezing amniotic fluid, her cells slowly changing and adapting to T-Veronica.

In the past year, however, that had changed. She had hypothesized that given enough time, T-Veronica would raise consciousness to new levels, expanding areas of the mind that would surpass simplistic human senses, and she had been correct. For the last ten months, she had begun experiencing herself in spite of stasis, testing her awareness . . . and she had been able to see through her human eyes, when she wished.

Alexia reached out with her mind and turned off the support machines. The tank began to drain, and she stared out at her dear brother, most unhappy that he had died. She could choose not to employ her emotions, but she had been human with him; it seemed appropriate.

When the tank was empty, Alexia opened it, stepping out into her new world. There was power everywhere, hers for the taking, but now she sat down in front of the tank and laid Alfred's bloody head in her lap, experiencing the sadness.

She began to sing, a child's song that her brother had liked, stroking his hair back from his drawn face. There was sadness in the lines around his eyes and mouth, and she wondered what his life had been like. She wondered if he'd stayed at Rockfort, stayed at Veronica's home, the home of their ancestors.

Still singing, Alexia reached out to her father—and was surprised to find him missing, either dead or beyond her range of perception. She had touched his mind only recently, studying what was left of it. In a way, he was responsible for what she had become; the T-Veronica had turned his mind to sludge, had driven him insane . . . as it would have to her, if she hadn't tested it on him, first.

She stretched her awareness, finding sickness and death in the upper levels of the terminal. A pity. She had been looking forward to beginning her experiments again, immediately; without test subjects, she had no reason to stay.

She found two people not far from the Umbrella facility and decided to flex her control over substance, to see how much effort it took—and found that it was hardly an effort at all. She concentrated for just a few seconds, saw a male and female inside of a snow machine, and wished for them to be brought back to the facility.

Instantly, lines of organic matter tore through the ice, ripping toward the vehicle. Amused, Alexia watched with her senses as a giant tentacle of new-formed substance rose up and curled around the machine, lifting it effortlessly into the air—and then threw it back at the facility. The machine tumbled end over end, its engine bursting into flame, and came to rest against one of the Umbrella buildings.

Both were still alive, she thought, and was well pleased. She could use one of them in an experiment she'd been thinking about for weeks, and would surely find a good use for the other in due time.

Alexia continued to sing to her dead brother, intrigued by the changes she could see coming, looking forward to gaining a fuller mastery of her new powers. She stroked his hair, dreaming.

Thirteen

THINGS FELL TO SHIT PRETTY FAST WHEN HE
finally reached the island.

Chris stood at the top of the cliff in the early night,
catching his breath and soundly cursing himself. Everything had been in that bag—weapons and ammo, rap-
pelling equipment so they could get back down to the
boat, flashlight, a basic first-aid kit, *everything*.

Not everything. *You've still got three grenades on your
belt,* his mind told him brightly. Terrific. Halfway up the
cliff he loses his grip and drops the bag into the deep
blue sea, but it appeared he still had his sense of humor.

*Yeah, that'll go a long way toward saving Claire's
life. Barry was right. I should have brought backup.*

Well. He could stand around all goddamn day wishing things were different, or he could get moving; he
picked moving.

Chris hunched over and stepped into the low cave entrance he'd chosen to start at, an isolated area but definitely connected to the rest of the compound—there was a radio antenna on the ledge outside, and when he straightened up a few steps later, he was inside a large, open room, the walls and ceiling organic but the floor carefully leveled.

There was light somewhere ahead, and Chris started for it, keeping his fingers crossed that he wasn't about to walk into an Umbrella Military dinner. He doubted it. From what he'd seen of the island, the attack Claire had mentioned had been excessively brutal.

He was less than a dozen steps into the shadowy chamber when a small tremor shook the cave, spilling rock dust and pebbles over his head—and closing the cave entrance he'd just walked through, collapsing rock having a fairly distinctive sound. It seemed the island attack had made things a bit unstable.

"Oh, wonderful," he muttered, but was suddenly a bit happier about the grenades. Not that they would help much here. Even if he could blow the mouth without bringing all of it down, it was still too high to jump, and the rope had been in the bag; unless she'd been taking lessons, Claire wasn't a good enough rock climber to go down unassisted—

"What?" someone rasped, and Chris dropped into a defensive crouch, searching the shadows—

—and saw a man on the cave floor, slumped against the wall. He wore a tattered white T-shirt with blood on it, his pants and boots military—he was one of Umbrella's, and not in very good shape. Nevertheless, Chris stepped quickly to his side, ready to kick the shit out of him if he so much as sneezed.

"I didn't know anyone was still around," the man said weakly, and coughed a little. "Thought I was the last one . . . after the self-destruct."

He coughed again, obviously not far away from death. His words sank in, creating a lead ball in Chris's stomach. Self-destruct?

He crouched down, trying to keep his voice level. "I'm here looking for a girl, her name is Claire Redfield. Do you know where she is?"

At the sound of Claire's name, the man smiled, though not at Chris. "An angel. She's gone, escaped. I helped her . . . let her go. She tried to save me, but it was too late."

Hope bloomed anew. "Are you sure she got away?"

The dying man nodded. "Heard the planes leave. Saw a jet come out of the basement, under the . . ." a cough, "the tank. You should go, too. Nothing left here."

Chris could feel some of his stress and fear ebbing away, tensions in his neck and back releasing. If she was gone, she was safe.

"Thank you for helping her," he said sincerely. "What's your name?"

"Raval. Rodrigo Raval."

"I'm Claire's brother, Chris," he said. "Let me help you, Rodrigo, it's the least I can do and—"

Eeaaaaaaa!

A deafening animal cry filled the cave, and at the same instant, another tremor struck, a bad one, the ground shaking so hard that Chris was thrown off his feet—

—and earth *erupted,* what Chris thought was an explo-

sion at first, a fountain of dirt and rock spraying upward—
but it kept rising, and Chris could see thick, filth-coated
slime beneath it, could smell sulfur and decay, saw a huge
cylinder made of rubber still climbing—

—and then it shrieked again, the top of the cylinder
twisting around, wormy tentacles peeling back from a
yawning, howling throat, and Chris scrambled to his
feet, grabbing a grenade from his belt—

—and the giant, shrieking snake-worm came crashing down, mouth open—

—and swallowed Rodrigo whole before slamming
into the sandy soil where he'd been sitting. It dove into
the ground like a swimmer into water, its impossibly
long body arching over, following through.

Jesus!

Chris stumbled away as the ground continued to
quake, the burrowing creature kicking up rock and dirt
and sand all around him, and he realized that he had to
kill it or get away fast, that it could easily come up beneath him for another quick snack.

He ran to the outer wall of the cave, making a split
second plan as the snake-worm burst up through the
ground behind him, its insane mouth peeling open as it
hesitated at the top of its arch, ready to plunge down
over him, rocks falling all around—

—and Chris pulled the safety ring off the grenade,
stripping the tape and pin away, and ran, straight for the
creature's lower body where it emerged from the ground.

Crazy, this is crazy—

He ducked just before hitting the filthy, muscular
body and set the grenade on the ground in front of it, on

the run, as careful as he could be not to set it off—and then dived for cover *behind* the snake-worm's twisting body, tucking into a shoulder roll, covering his head as the animal started downward, shrieking—

—and *BOOM,* the explosion shook the ground even harder than the animal had, the shriek cut off, the grenade blast muffled by a half ton of worm guts that shot out in all directions, stinking and warm, painting the walls of the cave in viscous bucket loads.

Chris rolled on his back, drenched, watched the front half of the animal convulse and writhe, already dead—and as its muscles and reflexes clenched and released for the last time, the snake-worm expelled a gush of stomach acid and rock from its gaping maw, vomiting out its last meal.

Rodrigo!

Before the massive corpse had completely settled to the ground, Chris was at Rodrigo's side, horrified and helpless, the man seizing in shock and pain. He was coated in yellow bile, and Chris could see places where it had already burned through his skin.

Rodrigo let out a soft cry, too weak to scream in what had to be incredible pain, and Chris tore his own jacket off, wiping his face clean of the sticky, acidic fluid.

"You're going to be okay, just relax, don't try to talk," Chris said, fully aware that Rodrigo would be dead in minutes, perhaps seconds. He kept talking, kept his tone soothing in spite of his own dismay.

Rodrigo opened his eyes, and though they were full of suffering, they also had the wet, glassy, faraway look of someone leaving it all behind, someone about to be free of pain and fear.

"Right . . . pocket . . ." Rodrigo whispered. "The angel . . . gave . . . for luck."

Rodrigo took a slow, deep breath, and let it out just as slowly, an exhalation that seemed to go on forever, and then he was gone.

Chris automatically closed his half-open eyes, simultaneously sad and relieved at Rodrigo's passing, the end of a life but also an end to dying.

Rest, friend.

Sighing, Chris reached into Rodrigo's pocket, felt skin-warmed metal—and pulled out the scuffed, heavy old lighter that he'd given to Claire himself, a long time ago. For luck.

Chris held it to his chest, suddenly overwhelmed by a rush of love for his sister. She'd carried the lighter with her everywhere for years, but had given it up to ease the mind of a dying man, possibly one of the men responsible for her capture.

He slipped it into his pocket and stood, glad that he'd be able to give it back to her—and to tell her that she'd made a difference in Rodrigo's last hours, that he'd smiled upon hearing her name. Even though Claire didn't need to be rescued, Chris's trip to the island had already turned out to be worthwhile.

The stink of the splattered cave was getting to him, and now that he knew his sister was safe, all that was left was to get himself home. His entrance had been caved in, and he didn't have a decent weapon, but if someone had triggered Umbrella's self-destruct system—it seemed that all their illegal facilities were built with such failsafes in place, a fine way to destroy evidence if anything went wrong—then he shouldn't run into too much trouble looking for the tank that Rodrigo had mentioned, see if there was another jet to be had.

"No going back," he said softly, and with a final silent prayer for Rodrigo to find peace, he went to see what he could find.

There was a fight about to happen on one of the monitors in what was left of the control room, and Albert Wesker, frustrated by a day of fruitless searching and not looking forward to yet another long flight, pulled up a crate and sat down to watch. He'd already sent the boys back to the world, he was alone—except it appeared that he'd missed somebody, and said somebody was still wandering around the island . . .

. . . *but not for much longer,* he thought happily, wishing the reception was better; thanks to that lonesome loser, Alfred Ashford, the self-destruct system had screwed everything up . . . and finally, something interesting was actually going to happen.

Christ, he's unarmed!

Crazy or stupid or totally ignorant of what the island was, no question. Wesker grinned. The unarmed man was walking through the training facility just one floor below, and he was about to meet up with one of Umbrella's newer bio-organics, one that had been trapped down in the sewers until Wesker had shown up and set it free. They were one hallway apart; when the dumbass turned the next corner, he was dead.

Wesker adjusted his sunglasses, pleasantly diverted from his own troubles. Sweepers, Umbrella was calling the new monsters, but they were basically Hunters with poison claws—huge, primarily amphibious, violent as hell. In Wesker's opinion, the Hunters, the 121 series, were perfectly badass without the extra poison touch.

But isn't that just like Umbrella, always wasting resources, playing games when they could be winning wars.

Yes, it was, but there was about to be bloodshed. Wesker set aside his distaste for the company and leaned in to watch.

The weaponless idiot—a tall guy with reddish-brown hair, that was about all the static would allow—was two steps from disaster, the Sweeper waiting just around the corner . . . when he stopped and backed up a step, pressing himself against the damaged wall.

Wesker frowned. The man started to back up, slowly and carefully, still hugging the wall. Okay, maybe not a *complete* idiot.

He'd made it halfway back down the corridor he'd come through when the Sweeper finally got impatient, deciding to take action. There was no sound system left, but the creature had thrown back its head and was screaming, that weird, trilling screech floating up to Wesker through the ruined building just a split second later.

"Get him," Wesker breathed eagerly, looking back at the poor, doomed dumbass . . . just in time to see him throwing something, something small and dark, the Sweeper leaping out from behind the corner, still screaming, the object landing at its feet—

—and the building was shaking, the screens going white and then black, the deep thunder of explosives rumbling through the floor.

Wesker was astounded. And then furious. That creature had been a miracle of science, a warrior created for battle—who was this dick who'd just rambled in and blown it to shit?

A dead dick, Wesker thought darkly, pushing the crate away and heading for the stairs. He took them two at a time, carefully bypassing a few still burning fires, aware that he was channeling all his frustrations and upsets toward the unknown soldier and not particularly caring. Alexia wasn't at Rockfort, which meant he had to get his ass to the Antarctic of all places, to the only other facility she might be at; why else would Alfred have gone there? And if Wesker didn't get to her before she woke up, he might have to go home empty handed . . . all of which added up to failure, and if there was one thing Wesker hated, it was losing.

He marched through the crumbling leftovers of the training facility, reaching the hall he wanted, silencing his steps as he edged farther along. There was still smoke in the air when he reached the corner where the conflict had taken place, but little left of the Sweeper. Most of it was stuck to the walls and ceiling.

There, ahead and to the left; he could smell the intruder, could smell sweat and anxiety emanating from the small working lab to which he'd retreated.

This is going to hurt you more than it hurts me, he thought, his mood lifting somewhat at the thought of a little personal interaction.

Not wanting to get blown up, Wesker didn't hesitate, didn't give the guy a chance to get paranoid. He strode into the room, saw the soon-to-be corpse standing with his back turned, and moved. Moved the way only he could move—one second, he was walking through the door, the next, he was spinning the intruder around, lifting him by his throat—

—and then looking into the startled face of Chris Redfield.

Oh, my.

Chris, who'd been on the Raccoon S.T.A.R.S., who'd been led—under Wesker's command—to the Spencer estate, where he'd proceeded to thoroughly screw up Wesker's plans. Chris Redfield had cost him money, had almost cost him his life—but worst of all, he had been primarily responsible for the biggest failure in Wesker's career.

Wesker recovered himself quickly, a dark, wonderful joy spreading through his entire body. "Chris Redfield, as I live and breathe—what brings you to Rockfort, if you don't mind me . . ."

Wesker trailed off, still gazing up into Redfield's increasingly red face as he uselessly pried at Wesker's fingers. The girl, of course! He hadn't even known that Chris *had* a sister, but the deranged letter that Alfred Ashford had so thoughtfully left behind explained everything . . . including his plans for the young Claire Redfield.

"She's not here," Wesker said, grinning. With his free hand, he straightened his sunglasses.

"You . . . you're dead," Chris gasped, and Wesker grinned wider, not bothering to respond to such a stupid statement.

"Don't change the subject, Chris. Don't you want to know where Claire is, hmmm? Did you know that her plane took a little unplanned detour to the Antarctic?"

Chris was slowly choking to death, but Wesker could see that the news of his sister was hitting him harder than his own imminent demise. *Wonderful!*

"There are experiments being performed there," Wesker mock-whispered, as if telling him a secret. "I plan on going myself, see if I can get an experiment or two of my own going . . . tell me, is your sister good-looking? Do you think she might be interested in getting some action, because I've got a hard-on like you wouldn't believe—"

Chris flailed at Wesker, the helpless fury in his eyes absolutely *gorgeous*. He hit Wesker in the face, knocking his sunglasses to the ground . . . and Wesker laughed, blinking up at him slowly, letting him see. He still wasn't used to it himself, the gold-red cat's eyes occasionally surprising him when he looked in a mirror—and they had exactly the effect he'd hoped for.

"What . . . *are* you?" Chris rasped out.

"I'm better, that's what," Wesker said. "New employers, you know. After the Spencer estate, I needed a little help getting back on my feet, which they were perfectly willing to provide. You think Claire will like it?"

"Monster," Chris spat.

I'll show you monster, you shit.

Wesker started to close his hand, slowly, watching Chris's eyes bulging, a vein on his forehead popping out—

—and was stopped by the sound of laughter. Cool, female laughter, filling the room, surrounding them.

"Don't you want to play with me?" a voice said, the same woman, low and sexy and dangerous, and then she began to laugh again, an unmerciful, beautiful sound that finally trailed away to nothing.

Alexia!

God, she was awake . . . and the kind of power it would take for her to look in on him here, to project herself so far . . .

Wesker threw Chris to one side, barely hearing the plaster wall crack beneath his useless skull, his thoughts full of Alexia. He had to go to her immediately. He had to have her, and not just for the sample . . . though he'd take what he could get.

"I'm coming," he said, scooping up his sunglasses and then *moving,* speeding through the broken facility to where his private plane waited. Chris Redfield was his past; Alexia Ashford meant his future.

Chris crawled to his feet soon after Wesker left, aching in about a dozen places, his throat horribly sore. He didn't know what had happened, exactly, didn't know who the woman was or why Wesker had seemed so eager to get to her—but he understood now who had attacked Rockfort, and suspected the reason. Albert Wesker should have died when the Spencer mansion had burned, but it seemed he'd sold his soul to someone new at the price of his life, someone obviously as nasty and amoral as Umbrella—someone who was perfectly willing to kill for whatever it was they wanted, for something that Umbrella had.

Chris didn't care. At the moment, all he cared about was Claire, and getting himself to this Antarctica facility. He knew that Umbrella had a legitimate base there . . . it had to be the same one, and if it wasn't, somebody there would know where the experiments *were* taking place.

He had one grenade left. If he could find the underground airport, he'd have no trouble getting inside, and he could fly anything with wings. He'd radio on the way for a read on the Umbrella base, and if he couldn't find a weapon to get her out, he'd use his bare hands.

All that mattered was Claire. And he was on his way.

FourTeen

THEY WERE MERE HOURS AWAY.

Two men connected by history, one her enemy, the other . . . Alexia didn't know about the other, not yet, but knew that he meant to reclaim the girl she'd taken from the snow machine. Probably the boy, as well. None of them would be leaving, of course . . . but she was looking forward to the petty intrigues and overblown, self-important dramas that their humanity would bring to her home. She would enjoy the chance to observe their natural tendencies and instincts before forever altering their lives.

She stood in the great hall considering things: possible futures, her next transformation, the structural and psychological changes her new synthesis would create in humans, how she should welcome her new guests . . . and it occurred to her that her home, deep beneath the ice and snow, might be difficult for them to achieve. She immediately wished for the doors to be opened, for obstacles to be removed . . . and she heard and saw and felt the result in the same instant, existing in a hundred places at once as locks were broken and walls were taken down, as debris was pushed aside and apertures were widened.

She was prepared. Things would move quickly now . . . and what happened in the next hours would, to a degree, define her choices for some time to come. It was all still so new, the templates of her new life written only in sand . . .

Smiling at her own poetic notions, Alexia went to see about the first series of injections for the boy.

FifTeen

Something was very, very wrong in Umbrella's Antarctica facility, but Chris didn't know what it was.

On the fifth basement level of the dark and deserted compound, hundreds of feet beneath the snow, Chris stood in front of what appeared to be a full-blown mansion made of white brick. There was a fountain behind him, potted plants, even a decorative merry-go-round. He'd been led there, presumably because someone wanted him to go inside, but he didn't know who or why.

His instincts were telling him to get the hell out, but he ignored them. He had to, not knowing if he was a lamb being led to slaughter or if he was being taken to Claire. Since landing the jet in the roof hangar, he'd been guided every step of the way—walking into halls and having doors lock behind him, others opening up in front of him . . . twice, he'd found jewels on the cold cement floors, pointing him in a particular direction, and once, after taking a wrong turn, all of the lights had gone out. They'd come back on when he'd groped his way back to where he'd gone "wrong."

It had been strange enough just getting to the facility, passing over the endless miles of gray ice and snow . . . and then seeing it for the first time, rising up from the blank plains like an illusion . . .

But to be herded someplace like an animal, shuffled along without knowing the reason . . .

Chris was scared, more scared than he wanted to admit. He'd tried to stop, to look around for weapons or clues, but everything had been shut off, every door he tried locked—except for the ones he was supposed to go through, of course. The cameras that had to be watching his every move were so well hidden that he hadn't seen even one of them . . . but it almost seemed that his shepherd knew his *mind,* knew what signals to give him, knew how to keep him going. He'd thought initially that it was Wesker, that it was all some setup to trap him— but why bother? He could have strangled Chris at the island if he'd wanted to. No, he was being guided for some other reason, and it seemed he had no choice but to follow along . . . not if he wanted to find Claire.

He took a deep breath and opened the front door of the mansion, stepping inside.

It was beautiful, as extravagant as the front of the building had suggested, grand staircase, arched pillars—and strangely familiar, though it took him a moment to see how, the colors and decorations different. It was the layout—the same basic layout as the front hall of the Spencer mansion. It was surreal, but so perfectly harmonious with all the other weirdness that he didn't bat an eye.

Chris stood for a moment, waiting, looking around for another signal—and then he heard what sounded like a laugh coming from behind the stairs. It was the same laugh that he'd heard at the Rockfort facility, that woman.

What had she said? Something about wanting to play?

It definitely felt like a game, like he was a character being moved around for someone else's enjoyment— and it was starting to piss him off. That he was afraid only made him angrier.

Chris stalked toward the back wall, ready to confront this woman, to demand some answers—

—but when he stepped around one of the decorative pillars, he saw that there was no one there.

"What the hell is this," he muttered, turning—

—and there was Claire. Webbed to the back of the stairs as if by some giant spider, her eyes closed, her head hanging limply.

Wesker wasn't surprised to find that parts of the Antarctic compound had been built to look like parts of the Spencer estate. The underground extravagance was an incredible waste, but as he'd noted many times before, so like Umbrella.

It was all about intrigue for them, back at the beginning. Before it all turned into a bad spy movie.

Oswell Spencer and Edward Ashford had been responsible for the creation of the T-virus, but it had been their only real accomplishment; the rest was money thrown away. Truly, the entire facility—except for the laboratories, of course—was an expensive joke, set up by old men and children with little imagination and too much money.

Aware that Alexia was probably watching, Wesker took his time, moving from level to level, clearing away a few wandering zombies as he walked. He wasn't carrying a weapon, had simply snapped their necks and left them to asphyxiate. Twice, he was spotted by other creatures, things he'd sensed and not seen, but they hadn't attacked, perhaps recognizing him as one of their own.

Wesker kept moving, sure that Alexia would find him when she was ready. He'd landed his jet some distance from the compound, wanting to be sure that she understood how he was different—that the elements didn't affect him, that he was physically stronger than any five men put together, with better endurance and sharper senses. He also wanted her to see that he was respectful of her space, that he was willing to be patient . . . and that he was extremely determined.

Whenever you want, my sweet, he thought, walking through a cold room corridor on the fifth basement floor. He'd been through the area already, but knew that the "mansion" was there, and suspected that she would want to greet him in high style. It didn't matter to him, she could drop in on him in a toilet stall for all he cared, but he thought she was probably as vain and spoiled as her brother. However powerful and brilliant she was, she was also a twenty-five-year-old rich girl who had spent fifteen of those years sleeping.

Rich, beautiful . . . playful. She probably didn't even

understand her powers yet, but it wouldn't be long now, he could feel it. He left the icy stillness of the cold corridor and started for the mansion once again.

Claire woke slowly, her aching body gently supported by warm hands that lifted and held her. She was laid down, the cold floor bringing her around, and when she opened her eyes, she saw her brother. Smiling at her.

"Chris!" She sat up and embraced him, ignoring her sore muscles, so happy to see him that for a moment, she forgot everything else. It was Chris, it was him, finally!

"Hey, sis," he said, fiercely hugging her back, the familiar sound of his voice making her warm and safe. She wished it could last forever, *after so long!*

"Claire . . . I think we ought to get out of here, now," he said, and she could hear a thread of concern behind his words that woke her up, that reminded her of all that had happened. "I don't know exactly what's going on, but I don't think it's safe."

"We have to find Steve," she said, and started to get to her feet, worried. Chris helped her, supporting her while she steadied herself.

"Who's Steve?"

"A friend," Claire said. "We got away from Rockfort together, and we were about to get away from here, too—but something . . . some kind of creature grabbed our snowmobile and threw it—"

She looked up at Chris, suddenly more than just worried. "Before I blacked out, I heard him say my name— he's alive, Chris, we can't leave him—"

"We won't," Chris said firmly, and Claire felt weak

with relief. Chris had come, he knew all about Umbrella, he'd be able to find Steve and take them away—

Laughter. A woman was laughing, a high, cruel laugh. Chris stepped out from behind the stairs, Claire following, both of them looking up to the balcony, and there was the woman, it was—

Alfred?

No, not Alfred. And that meant . . .

"There really is an Alexia," Claire said softly. *Go goddamn figure.*

Still laughing, Alexia Ashford turned and walked away, exiting through a door at the top of the stairs.

"She might know where Steve is," Chris said urgently, even as it occurred to Claire, and then both of them were running, climbing, Claire quickly outpacing him, ready to slap the truth out of Alfred's creepy sister—

—and *CRASH,* behind her, the stairs falling away, Claire rolling to the floor as a huge tentacle smashed through the balcony, *like in the snow cat*—

—and then it was gone, retreating through the hole it had created, leaving a trashed set of side stairs behind. The main staircase was still whole, but Claire was stuck on the second floor on a shattered wood island. She'd have to climb down.

"Claire!"

She crawled to her feet, saw Chris down below, wincing at some pain in his leg amid the broken wood and plaster.

"Are you okay?" Claire asked, and Chris nodded— and then there was a scream, and she felt her blood run cold.

It came from beyond the door that Alexia had gone

through, and it was Steve, there was no question in Claire's mind. It was Steve, and he was in pain.

Can't leave Chris, but—

"Chris, it's him," Claire said, looking between her brother and the door, not sure what to do.

"Go, I'll catch up!" Chris called.

"But—"

"Go! I'll be fine, just be careful!"

Terrified, Claire turned and ran, hoping she wasn't too late.

Wesker stepped into the grand foyer of the underground mansion, and saw it wasn't quite so grand anymore. Something had happened to the stairs, part of the upper balcony now smashed to the floor.

He heard someone moving around behind a huge, jagged piece of balcony still hanging from the tattered carpet, and took a step toward it—

—and there she was. Standing at the top of the stairs in a long, dark dress, silky blond hair tied back from her pale, beautiful face.

"Alexia Ashford," Wesker said, surprised to find himself somewhat in awe now that the moment was at hand. She looked human, delicate and helpless, but he knew better.

Make your pitch, and make it good.

Wesker cleared his throat, stepping forward and taking off his sunglasses. "Alexia, my name is Albert Wesker. I represent a group who has long admired your work, and have been eagerly awaiting your, ah, return."

She watched him impassively, head tilted slightly, her

back straight and stiff. She looked like a debutante at her first society party.

"And may I add that it's a personal honor to meet you," Wesker said sincerely. "My employers told me all about you. I know your father sired you with the genes of his own great-great grandmother, Veronica—that with her genetic material, the very foundation of the Ashford line, he created you and Alfred to be the culmination of genius. Veronica would surely be proud.

"I know you created T-Veronica in her honor . . ." careful, he probably shouldn't mention what had happened to her father, *don't bitch this up*, ". . . and that you are the only, ah, being alive with access to the virus."

"I am the virus," Alexia said coolly, studying him through narrowed eyes.

"Yes, of course," Wesker said. God, he hated this diplomatic shit, he was terrible at it, but he wanted to impress her, to impress *upon* her how valuable she was to certain interested parties.

"So," he continued, thinking how much easier things would have been if he'd gotten to her in stasis, "I would like it very much—we would all appreciate it if you would agree to accompany me to a private meeting with my employers, to discuss an alliance of sorts. I can assure you that you won't be disappointed."

She waited to see if he was finished—and then laughed, long and loud. Wesker felt himself flush. It was clear from her tone exactly what she thought of his request.

Fine. Nice time is over.

Wesker stepped forward and held out his hand. "We

want a sample of T-Veronica," he said, the gloss disappearing from his voice. "And I'm going to have to insist that you give it to me."

As she started down the stairs, for just a second he thought she was going to do it—but then she started to change, and he stopped thinking anything. He could only stare, his awe returning tenfold.

A step down, and her dress burned away in searing veins of golden light, the light coming from her body. Another step, and her flesh changed, turned a deep gray, her hair disappearing, gray flesh locks growing from the top of her head and flopping down to frame her face. Her nakedness was transformed with her next step, as rough, pebbled armor grew over one leg and her groin, curled up to support a rounded breast, to cover her right arm. By the time she reached the bottom of the stairs, she no longer resembled Alexia Ashford.

His breath taken away, Wesker reached for her—and with the back of her hand, she struck him, and then he was flying, landing in a heap by the front door.

Such power!

He stood up, understanding that force might be useful, and prepared himself to *move,* to use his own power—

—and with a smile, she waved her hand and fire burst up from the marble floor, lines of it surrounding him, beckoned to life by her slender fingers. She lowered her hand and the flames went down but didn't die, still burning from stone, from bare stone.

Wesker knew then that it was over. If she chose to spare him, he'd be lucky. Without another word, he turned and walked out, running as soon as the door had closed behind him.

The part-creature left, and only seconds later, the young man followed, believing that he'd escaped unseen. Alexia watched them run, amused but slightly disappointed. She'd expected more.

The part-creature was no threat, and she decided to spare him. His arrogance had pleased her, if not his pathetic "offer." The young man, though . . . brave and self-sacrificing, loyal, compassionate. Physically, a good specimen. And he loved his sister, who was about to die—it would make for an interesting physiological reaction.

Alexia decided that she would create a confrontation for them to interact. She would test a new form for herself and see if his grief made him bolder, or if it proved to be a liability—

She laughed, suddenly imagining a suitable, an *apt* form to take. Except for Alfred, no one had known the simple secret of T-Veronica, that it was based on the chemistry of a queen ant. She would try an insectile configuration, experience the strengths and advantages that such a form would propose.

Her disappointment was past. The girl and her boy would die, and then she would indulge herself with the young man.

Sixteen

THROUGH THE ROOMS AND HALLS OF A MAN-
sion, Claire had run, afraid to hear him scream again,
afraid not to because she didn't know where to look.
Past the plushly decorated halls she found herself in a
prison area, cells on either wall, the environment cold
and dark once more. A lone virus carrier reached for her
from behind bars, wailing.

"Steve!"

Her voice echoed back at her, full of tension and fear,
but Steve didn't answer. There was a thick metal door to
her right, different than the others, reinforced by bands
of steel. She opened it, stepping into a small, bare room
that opened into a much larger one.

"Steve!"

No answer, but the bigger room was long and dimly
lit, a kind of huge hall, and she couldn't see what was at

the other end. She saw that there was a suspended gate between the small room and the hall, which definitely gave her pause. She looked around and found a piece of broken wood on the floor, then wedged it between the outer door and its frame, not wanting to end up locked inside.

She hurried into the giant hall, intimidating, over-sized statues of knights lining the heavily shadowed walls, her anxiety growing with every passing second. Where was he, why had he screamed?

She was halfway down the hall when she saw him, slumped in a chair at the far end, some kind of restraining bar across his chest.

Oh, God . . .

Claire ran, and as she got closer she could see that the bar was a huge ax, a halberd, the blade firmly entrenched in the wall next to him. He seemed very small and very young, his eyes closed and head down—but she could see that he was breathing, and felt less anxious.

She reached his side and pulled at the giant ax, but it wouldn't budge. She crouched next to him, touching his arm, and he stirred, opened his eyes.

"Claire!"

"Steve, thank God you're all right, what happened? How did you get here?"

Steve pushed at the long ax handle but couldn't move it either. "Alexia, it had to be Alexia, she looked just like Alfred—she injected me with something, she said she was going to do what she'd done to her father, but she was going to get it right this time—"

He shoved at the ax again, straining, but it wasn't

moving. "In other words, she was whacked. I guess she and Alfred were pretty close after all . . ."

Steve trailed off, his cheeks suddenly flushing with color. His hands started to twitch, his body trembling.

"What is it?" Claire asked, afraid, so afraid, because his body was hunching over, his fingers clenching to fists, his eyes wild and terrified.

"Cuh . . . Claire . . ."

His voice dropped an octave, her name becoming a growl, and then he was writhing in the chair, his clothes ripping. He opened his mouth and a liquid moan came out, frightened at first but then angry. Furious.

"No," Claire whispered, started to back away, and Steve grabbed the halberd, wrenching it out of the wall, standing up. His body continued to hunch over, his head dropping down, muscles rippling beneath skin that was turning a gray green. Spikes rose up from his left shoulder, two, three of them, as his hands elongated, as a giant, bloodless wound grew across his back, as his eyes turned red and animal.

The thing that had been Steve Burnside opened its mouth and screamed, enraged, and Claire turned and sprinted away, sick with loss and fright, running for all she was worth.

The monster came after her, swinging the massive ax, the sharp edge whistling through the air. She could feel the wind from the swinging blade and somehow found more speed, her legs pumping, pushing her faster.

The monster swung again, hit something, the sound vast and deafening. Faster, faster, the small room just ahead—

—and the gate was coming down, was about to lock

her into the hall with the monster, *how,* didn't matter, she had to go faster still or she was dead—

—and with one final, brutal push, Claire dove for the shrinking space between the bottom of the gate and the floor, sliding in on her stomach, the gate crashing closed behind her.

The monster roared, began swinging the ax with abandon, sparks flying as it attacked the metal bars. In shock, Claire watched it break through three of them, bending the steel by the very ferocity of its blows, before she realized she could get out.

Door, I propped the door open, she thought dazedly, and stood up, took a single step toward her escape—

—and then something broke through the wall with a *crash,* not the monster, a thing that wrapped around her like a constrictor, lifting her, another of the tentacles. The monster continued to hack at the metal, it would break through in seconds, and the tentacle had her tightly in its rubbery grasp.

Awakened from her daze, Claire beat at her captor, pried at it, but the matter was impervious. It simply held her, waiting for the monster to breach the gate.

It wanted to beat her and cut her, it wanted to rip her apart, so it slammed the weapon into the bars over and over, and finally, there was a hole it could pass through.

She was making noises in the grip of the thing that held her, gasping noises that made its blood hot and excited, that made it raise the ax, lusting for the end of her.

It brought the ax down, hard, remembering what he'd told her, promised her—

—you can get the next one—

—I will—

—and it, he, stopped, the blade almost touching her skull. The tentacle waited, gripped her tighter, and he remembered.

Claire.

Steve lifted the ax again, strong, he was so strong, and slammed it down into the tentacle, slicing through.

In a spray of green fluid, the thick coil snapped and hit him in the chest, throwing him into the wall before retreating. He felt and heard ribs break, felt the boil of his blood cooling, felt his strength going away.

The pain came, sharp and dull and everywhere, but he opened his eyes and she was there, she was safe, she was reaching for his hand. Claire Redfield, reaching for his hand with tears in her eyes.

The monster was gone.

She reached out to hold his hand and he lifted it to his face, to his beautiful, dying face, laying it across his cheek.

"You're warm," he whispered.

"Hang on," she said, pleading, the knot in her throat choking her, "please, my brother came and he'll take us with him, please don't die!"

Steve's eyes were fluttering, as though he were trying very hard to stay awake.

"I'm glad your brother came," he whispered, his voice fading. "And I'm glad I met you. I . . . I love you."

On the last word, his head fell forward, his chest falling and not rising again, and then Claire was alone.

Steve was gone.

Seventeen

CHRIS RAN, KNOWING THAT THEIR TIME WAS
short as long as Alexia Ashford was alive, afraid that she
might already have gotten to Claire.

"Claire!" he shouted, banging his fist on every door
he passed. It didn't matter, his shouting; if Alexia was
even half as powerful as he suspected, she already knew
where he was . . . and where Claire was.

Please, please don't hurt her, he thought, the thought
repeating itself as he ran down another hall, through a
door, another hall, and another. He didn't know if anything could stop Alexia, but if he could find Claire and
get them to the evac elevator, he meant to try and trigger
the self-destruct system before leaving. Alexia was
halfway to omnipotence and purely evil, she was an
apocalypse waiting to happen, and she had to be stopped.

"Claire!"

Through a familiar hallway, another Spencer estate copy, through a door that opened into some kind of shadowy prison, holding cells lining the walls. He had to find her, if he couldn't, he couldn't leave. He wanted Alexia dead, but he wouldn't endanger Claire's life, not for anything, and getting her out took absolute priority—

—and somebody was crying behind one of the closed doors. Chris stopped running and listened, trying not to breathe, tuning out the relentless banging of a virus carrier locked in another cell. Another gasping wail . . .

Claire, oh, thank God you're alive!

He ripped open the door, ready to hurt anything even close to her—and saw her sitting on the floor, sobbing, her arms wrapped around a young man, his naked body bruised and pitiful. He was dead.

Ah, shit.

It could only be Steve, Claire's friend, and though he was sorry for the boy he'd never met, Chris's heart was breaking for her. She looked so fragile, so alone . . . something else to lay at Alexia's doorstep. Chris had no doubt that Steve had died because of that crazy bitch. But as much as he wanted to sit down and comfort Claire, to hold her hand and let her grieve, he knew they had to get out.

"We have to go now, Claire," he said, as gently as possible—and was relieved when she nodded, carefully laying her friend down, closing his eyes with one trembling hand. She kissed him on the forehead and then stood up.

"Okay," she said, nodding again. "I'm ready."

She didn't look back, and in spite of everything, he was proud of her. She was strong, stronger than he would have been if he'd been asked to leave someone he'd cared about.

Together, they ran back into the hall, Chris figuring that they had to be close to the southwest corner of the building, where he'd landed the jet and seen the emergency evacuation elevator. The self-destruct system was presumably close enough to the elevator to make a fast escape possible; if they could just get to that elevator, he'd check every floor on the way up.

There were stairs at the south end of the hall, and Chris ran for them, Claire at his side. He could feel the seconds ticking past as they hurried up the steps, felt like time was closing in on them, that Alexia was finished playing.

Through the door at the top of the stairs, running out onto a giant metal grid platform—and Chris laughed out loud when he looked behind them, saw the nondescript doors of the emergency elevator.

"What?" Claire asked.

He motioned at the doors, grinning. "That'll take us straight to the jet."

Claire nodded, not smiling but she looked relieved. "Good. Let's go."

Chris had turned back to look at the wall across from the lift. "I've got to check something first," he said, wanting to take a closer look at the corner door, it looked like a security door. "You go, I'll be right there."

"Forget it," Claire said firmly. She walked after him, her eyes red from crying but her chin set and determined. "No way we're splitting up again."

Chris leaned down to look at the door's locking mechanism and sighed, standing back up. They were probably at the self-destruct system already; the lock was complicated and unique, requiring a key he didn't have. Besides which, to the right of the door was a locked-down grenade launcher of some kind, one he didn't recognize, the bar holding it down labeled *emergency release only.*

Just as well, we should get out while we still can, he thought, but wasn't happy about it. How much more powerful would Alexia become before another chance like this one?

"Hey—hey, wait a sec," Claire said, and began rummaging through the small pack around her waist. Before he could ask, she was holding up a slender metal key, shaped like a dragonfly. There was no question that it would fit the lock.

"I found it back at Rockfort," she said, bending over and pressing it into the indentation. It fit perfectly, the lock releasing with a solid metallic *clink.*

"You're going to set off the self-destruct, aren't you," Claire said, not really a question. "Do you have the code?"

Chris didn't really answer, thinking that there were an amazing number of coincidences in life, and sometimes, they worked to one's advantage.

"Code Veronica," he said softly, and pulled the door open, ready to take it all down, understanding that it was meant to be.

EIGHTEEN

THE BOY WAS DEAD, BUT THE GIRL WASN'T.
And now the young man was trying to destroy Alexia's
home, and it wasn't a game or an experiment or something to observe, he had to die, in pain and misery. How
had he dared to consider such a thing? He should be on
his knees in front of her, a worthless supplicant for her
to do with as she wished, how *dare* he?

Alexia saw the siblings walking away from their
treacherous deed, felt them wishing to leave as the auto-
mated sequence began, lights and sounds flashing, sys-
tems shutting down throughout the terminal. Their
perfidy was useless, of course. She would be able to
stop the destruct sequence with a minimum of effort,
using her control over the organic to sever every connection in the facility, but it was the thought behind the
act that so infuriated her. He had witnessed the glory of

her capabilities, he had seen it and fled in terror . . . and yet he could fancy himself worthy to take a life such as hers?

Alexia gathered herself, drawing all of her power in, becoming complete. She knew that the young man had picked up a weapon that had been sitting next to the keyboard, a revolver that someone had left behind. She didn't object, knowing that the firearm would give him hope, and that for a victory to be complete, the victor had to take everything. She would take his hope, she would take his sister's life and then she would take his.

When she was whole, she imagined herself becoming liquid, traveling through the structure of her surroundings as easily as the organic extensions she controlled, and then she was doing so, moving to confront the interlopers.

They were startled, as if they'd expected to succeed. She slid out from inside her organic carrier, unfolding herself, turning to look into their dull eyes, their wincing sheep's faces. She watched them watch her, curious in spite of her anger.

They argued in front of her, he insisting that he would "handle" things, that the girl should flee. The girl accepted, but reluctantly, insisting in turn that he should survive. Following that ludicrous statement, the girl turned and ran for the elevator.

Alexia moved to intercept, raising her hand to smite the girl—

—and a perforation opened in her flesh, distracting her. A bullet had entered her body. She turned and smiled at him, at the gun in his hand, and reached into herself, pulling the bullet out and tossing it toward him.

S.D. PERRY

As gratifying as his expression was, the girl was gone by the time she turned back.

It was time to expand her boundaries, Alexia decided. To show him what she was, what she could do . . . and to put the fear of God into him, because as she closed her eyes, imagining, wishing, she stopped being Alexia Ashford and became Wrath, divine and merciless.

Nineteen

"THE SELF-DESTRUCT SEQUENCE HAS BEEN activated," a recording intoned, reverberating through the room, crowding out the rest of its message. "You have four minutes thirty seconds to reach minimum safe distance." Combined with the sirens and flashing emergency lights, Chris was on sensory overload before the fight even began.

Alexia raised her hand to hit Claire, and Chris fired, the .357 bucking in his hand, the shot blasting over the self-destruct alarms, deafeningly explosive.

Yes! A clean hit, right through the gut, and Claire was already at the elevator, pushing the button, stepping inside—

—but instead of bleeding, instead of faltering even a step, Alexia smiled at him. She lifted one of her slender gray hands and pushed it into her body, the flesh melding seamlessly, flowing like water. A second later she held up the round he'd nailed her with and gently tossed it in his direction.

Bad, this is very, very bad, Chris thought numbly, and then she started to change.

The lithe gray female crouched on the metal grid and her liquid flesh started to tremble, to form tiny peaks and dips all across her body, the tissue bubbling, expanding. The peaks became mountains, the dips, valleys, all of it gray and swelling as her limbs started to fold in on themselves. Her arms curved over and joined the growing mass, the legs disappearing into it, the texture turning rough and striated, veins like cables rising, and she kept swelling. Her head rolled down and became part of the giant, rounded body of her, gray becoming muscle-tissue red, the purple and blue of blood vessels networking across like a tide.

"You have four minutes to reach minimum safe distance," someone said, but Chris barely heard her, he was backing away, becoming more and more convinced that this was not going to end well. The elevator was blocked, and she just kept getting bigger.

Thick tentacles pushed out from beneath the elephantine mass, undulating like waves, spreading out across the platform. Chris's back hit a wall, stopping him, and the thing, the massive, tumorous thing suddenly rose up as if unbending from some non-existent waist, spreading giant wings, a dragonfly's wings, raising a contorted and deformed half human face.

The face opened its mouth and a gigantic roaring shriek spilled out, the wings trembling from the raw power of the sound—and then it spit at him, a thin stream of yellow green bile that splashed on the platform at his feet, and began to eat through the metal.

"Shit!" Chris shouted, and barely jumped out of the way as one of the tentacles slashed forward. He had to watch the mouth and tentacles at the same time—

—and from rounded, quivering pink spheres that had grown up around the base of the giant body, moving things began to crawl out.

Chris ran to the farthest corner from the Alexia-thing and raised the .357, not sure where to shoot. The small subcreatures were landing on the platform, some like flat, rounded rocks with tentacles, some like beetles, some like nothing he'd ever seen before, and they were all coming toward him, moving fast.

The eyes, if you can't kill it maybe you can blind it— but the eyes were already blind, round gray holes with darkness underneath, and he'd already seen how effective bullets were against her flesh.

That decided it for him. Chris took aim and fired—

—and the pulsating, bloated creature was screaming again, this time in pain, one of her wings fluttering down to the platform.

A few of the small organisms had reached him, one of the beetle creatures leaping onto his leg, trying to climb up. Disgusted, he brushed it off, but there was another to take its place, and a third. A tentacle flew at his face, shot from one of the rounded stone shapes. Chris blocked it, but barely.

Move!

"You have three minutes thirty seconds to reach minimum safe distance."

Chris ran along the back wall, reached the other corner in front of the creature and targeted again, trying for another wing. The shot went high, but the next one hit.

It howled, the broken wing hanging from shredded connecting tissue, and then spit again, the stream of bile missing his face by inches. The thing now had only its two uppermost wings, and though he knew he'd hurt it, it didn't seem to have suffered anything close to serious injury.

And I have two rounds left.

There had to be something he could do, some way to stop it, the self-destruct was going to blow all of them to hell and it would be his fault. He leaped away as another tentacle whipped out from the creature's base, trying to think, this was a goddamn emergency and he had to *think*—

—*emergency release only.*

The bloated monster shrieked. More of the beetles were jumping at him but he ignored them, having only to turn his head to see the inset weapon next to the door, the one with the lockdown bar. A grenade or rocket launcher, whatever it was, it was beautiful, but the bar was still down, it hadn't released.

"You have two minutes to reach minimum safe distance."

Ka-chunk.

The bar flipped up.

Chris snatched it out, lifting and aiming it at the creature's swollen guts. He didn't know what it would do but he hoped it was good, he hoped it would shut that bitch *down.*

There was no safety, nothing to chamber. Chris pulled the trigger—

—and a fury of white light and heat leaped from the barrel, blowing into the fat belly like an arrow into a balloon. The effect was huge, the explosion monstrous.

A fountain of blood and gray jelly *splatted* out from the gaping, ragged hole, backsplattering onto his face, but he only had eyes for the screaming Alexia beast as its flesh and bone form gave out, deflating—

The upper body of the creature was trying to pull free from the dying mass, the two wings flailing frantically at the air, but with only two, it couldn't free itself . . . and so it was dying, he knew because he could see its blood draining away, because the color of its horrid flesh was changing, turning ashy, the subcreatures shriveling, because of the absolute, complete hatred on its face . . . and the absolute surprise.

As the Alexia monster fell silent and began to sag, her features dripping, Chris heard that he had one minute left.

Claire.

He dropped the incendiary launcher and ran.

Twenty

CLAIRE FELT LIKE SHIT, AND THERE WAS nothing she could do about it. Steve was dead, and Chris would either come or he wouldn't, and whatever happened, everything was going to blow up pretty soon, and she had no say in any of it.

"You have two minutes to reach minimum safe distance," the computer politely informed her, and Claire extended her middle finger toward the closest speaker. If there was a hell, she knew what they played in the elevators instead of music.

There was only one jet where the elevator had let her out, and Claire sat on the railing in front of it, her arms tightly crossed, her stare fixed on the elevator doors. She watched and waited, her anxiety building, a part of her believing completely that he wasn't coming as alarms blared through the mostly empty hanger, echoing back at her.

Don't leave me, Chris, she thought, clutching herself tighter. She thought of Steve, remembering the laugh attack he'd inspired back on the island. How he'd looked at her like she was crazy.

Come now, *Chris,* she thought, closing her eyes and wishing it as hard as she could. She couldn't lose him, too, her heart wouldn't be able to stand it.

There was one minute to reach minimum safe distance.

When the building started to rumble beneath her feet, she thought she might cry, but there were no tears. She went back to watching the elevator door instead, certain now that he was gone—so sure that when the door opened, when he stepped out, she thought she might be hallucinating.

"Chris?" she asked, her voice barely a whisper, and he was running toward her, splashes of blood and something else smeared across his face and arms, and that was when she understood that he was real. She wouldn't have hallucinated him with goop on his face.

"Chris!"

"Get in," he commanded, and Claire jumped into the second seat, happy and scared and anxious, lonely and relieved, wishing that Steve was with them and sad that he wasn't. There were more feelings, seeming dozens, but at the moment, she couldn't handle any of them. She pushed them aside and didn't think at all, didn't feel anything but hope.

Chris tucked them in tight and started pushing buttons, the small jet roaring to life. Above them, the ceiling slid apart, the storm clouds breaking up overhead as he lifted them out of the hanger, smooth and easy. A few seconds later, they were blasting away, leaving the dying facility behind.

Chris's shoulders relaxed, and he wiped his hand across his forehead, trying to rub off the sour-smelling gunk.

"I could use a shower," he said lightly, and the tears finally welled up, spilling over her lower lashes.

Chris, I thought I'd lost you, too . . .

"Don't leave me alone again, okay?" she asked, doing what she could to keep the tears out of her voice.

Chris hesitated, and she instantly knew why, knew that it wasn't over for either of them. That was too much to ask.

"Umbrella," she said, and Chris was nodding.

"We have to settle this, once and for all," he said tightly. "We have to, Claire."

Claire didn't know what to say, finally opting not to say anything. When the explosion came a moment later, she didn't look. She closed her eyes instead, leaning back into her seat, and hoped that when she finally slept, she wouldn't dream.

EPILOGUE

MILES AWAY, WESKER HEARD THE EXPLOSION, and could see the smoke rising shortly afterward, thick black plumes of it. He thought about circling the jet back, but decided against it; there was no point. If Alexia wasn't dead, his people would find out soon enough; hell, the *world* would find out soon enough.

"I hope you were in there, Redfield," he said softly, smiling a little. Of course he was; Chris wasn't bright enough or fast enough to have gotten out in time . . .

. . . *although he might be lucky enough.*

Wesker had to concede that much; Redfield had the luck of the devil.

It was a shame about Alexia turning him down. She'd been something, terrifying and evil, but definitely something. His employers weren't going to be happy when he came back without her, and he couldn't blame them; they'd shelled out plenty for the Rockfort attack, and he'd practically promised them results.

They'll live. If they don't like it, they can find themselves a new boy. Trent, on the other hand . . .

Wesker grimaced, not looking forward to their next meeting. He owed the man. After the Spencer fiasco, Trent had—quite literally—pulled his ass out of the fire, and arranged for him to be fixed up, better than new. And he'd been responsible for Wesker's introduction to his current employers, men with real aspirations for power, and the means to obtain it.

And . . .

And he'd never admit to it out loud, but Trent scared him. He was so smooth, well-mannered and soft-spoken—but with a glitter in his eyes that made him always seem to be laughing, like everything was a joke and he was the only one who got it. In Wesker's experience, the ones who laughed were the most dangerous; they didn't feel like they had anything to prove, and were usually at least slightly insane.

I'm just glad we're on the same side, Wesker assured himself, believing it because he wanted to. Because going up against someone like Trent was a bad, bad plan.

Well. He could worry about Trent later, after he'd made the proper apologies to the proper agents. At least Boyscout Redfield was dead, and he was still alive and kicking, working for the side that was going to win when all was said and done.

Wesker smiled, looking forward to the end. It was going to be spectacular.

The sun had come out and was reflecting against the snow, creating a brilliant radiance, blinding in its perfection. The small plane shot away, its shadow chasing it across the sparkling plains.

About the Author

S.D. (Stephani Danelle) Perry writes multimedia novel-izations in the fantasy/science-fiction/horror realm for love and money. In addition to the *Resident Evil* series, she is the bestselling author of *Avatar*, the two-volume relaunch of the *Star Trek: Deep Space Nine*® novels, which begins the arc of stories set after the TV series; and, *Star Trek-Section 31: Cloak*. She's also a two-time contributor to the acclaimed short story anthology, *Star Trek: The Lives of Dax*. Her other works include several *Aliens* novels, as well as the novelizations of *Timecop* and *Virus*. Under the name Stella Howard, she's written an original novel based upon the television series *Xena, Warrior Princess*. She lives in Portland, Oregon, with her husband and beloved dogs.